A Recipe
for
Romance

A COLLECTION OF 22
INSPIRATIONAL STORIES AND
RECIPES

Edited by Dana Corbit Nussio

DEDICATION

To the mothers, daughters, sisters and grandmothers – and,
yes, the fathers, brothers and sons – who read and celebrate
inspirational romance. We are blessed to have the opportunity
to share the stories of our hearts with you. And to Our Father
in Heaven, who makes all things possible – even the hope of
lifetime love.

INTRODUCTION

"You should eat the fruit of the labor of your hands; you shall be happy, and it shall be well with you." – Psalm 129:2 (RSV)

Family, faith and food – these three things just belong together. If you doubt this truth, you need only to attend a single church dinner to see the light as you breathe in the delicious aromas of prized recipes, bask in the warmth of family and then sample some of the best home cooking this side of Heaven.

As inspirational romance authors from Harlequin's Love Inspired, Love Inspired Historical and Love Inspired Suspense lines, we write stories of faith and family, with plenty of food on the table. So the idea of joining with our sister authors to present a charity anthology of short stories and recipes came as naturally as our next tales of forever love.

In each selection, you will find a romantic and family-friendly story and the chance to meet a new author or get to know one of your favorites better as she shares a favorite recipe and a little of herself. The authors in this collection represent fifteen states and two countries, and their stories – historical and contemporary romances and even some with a little suspense – are as different as the authors who wrote them. The recipes themselves are divided into three sections: Salads/Sides/Soups, Main Dishes and Desserts/Treats.

So we invite you to step inside these pages, pull up a chair and enjoy these sweet, mini-vacations into romance. Then try out the recipes a little later for a return trip to these Happily-Ever-Afters.

CONTENTS

SALADS/SIDES/SOUPS

SECOND CHANCE IN THE NORTHWOODS

BY LYN COTE

Heading to a job interview at 9 a.m., through the thick green forests of far northern Wisconsin to Rhinelander, Carrie couldn't shake the feeling that people were watching.

She knew it wasn't true. But she was hiding the truth, afraid someone would find out. She turned off Highway 47. Ahead, she saw the sign along Lincoln Street for MIKE'S AUTO REPAIR. Her heart pounded at the thought of what this job could mean for her. If she didn't find work, and soon, she wouldn't be able to stay here near . . . She slowed.

A horn beeped behind her, prompting her to turn in. She pulled up to the area near the door. Already the sound of tools emanated from within. Two bay doors stood open. She got out of the car, pressing down her bad case of nerves. Most of the time she felt as if she'd accomplished a lot in the past two years. Now that feeling deserted her.

She entered the building. The desk was unattended. Of course. She was here to apply for the position of receptionist and parts manager. She shifted, uneasy about what to do.

Finally, she walked to the door marked "Shop" and opened it.

The noise level shot up. She stood at the doorway, debating the best way to get someone's attention. A German shepherd stood up and walked slowly toward her. A guard dog? Her alarm rose.

Then the power drill, or whatever it was, stopped. A mountain of a man – Mike? –climbed out from beneath a vehicle on the hoist. She gasped, and her back bumped against the door.

In worn jeans and a gray T-shirt with "Mike's Auto" on it, Mike commanded attention. He moved with a grace she didn't expect from such a large man. Then she glimpsed his deep-brown eyes, his gentle gaze telling her not to be afraid. Jeannie had assured her that the Becks had lived in this area forever and were good people.

"Hi, I'm Mike Beck. Are you Carrie Baker? Jeannie McClure's friend?" He wiped his hands on a towel attached to his belt. The dog moved to his side, the animal's sharp eyes trained on her.

It still pained her that no one knew Jeannie was more than her friend. She cleared her throat. "Yes."

The man's large, slightly greasy hand gripped hers and shook it vigorously. The dog woofed once in welcome.

"Glad you could come. I didn't want to advertise if I could find someone who knew someone. I heard about you when I took Greta to Jeannie's husband, the vet."

Greta sat back on her haunches, panting.

Carrie's head swam with all of those connections. She'd grown up in a large city, feeling invisible, but here it seemed everybody knew everybody.

Then Greta lifted a paw toward her. Carrie automatically shook it, watching the big man beam at his pet.

Mike tried not to stare, but this young woman with long dark hair was so pretty and looked so nervous. "I hear you qualify as an executive assistant?"

Her head bobbed.

"Great! You need to fill out an application and then start

work."

Her eyes widening, Carrie didn't immediately respond. It must have been tough for her trying to get settled among strangers. The vet's wife had told him Carrie was shy. Or maybe his size made her nervous like it had others.

"Start?" she squeaked.

"Sure. If you want the job, it's yours."

Carrie hid her surprise as best she could and hurried to keep up with her new boss. And that's how she got the job at Mike's Auto Repair.

Weeks later

Carrie forced herself to sit on her hands. She'd given up the nasty habit of biting her nails. *And I won't start again.*

Mike walked in from the shop with his faithful sidekick, Greta, beside him. He stopped and studied Carrie, and the dog did the same. "You look upset."

She tried to think of some everyday reply. But none came. "I need to buy birthday presents."

His eyebrows rose. "Whose birthday?"

"My . . . the twins." The words were out before she could hold them back.

"You mean Jeannie's twins?"

"Jeannie's twins," she echoed, grateful to be misunderstood. No one here knew the truth. No one would for a long time. "I don't know what to get them."

She didn't know why she was telling him that either. He was an unmarried man without kids. But somehow easygoing Mike invited confidences.

Mike appeared to consider what she'd told him before picking up his phone and punching in a number. "Hey, Mom. My receptionist, Carrie Baker, needs help with buying birthday gifts."

He handed Carrie the phone, then settled into one of the waiting room chairs, petting the dog as it leaned against his thigh. Surprised, Carrie accepted the receiver.

"Hello, Mrs. Beck."

4

"Call me Kerry Ann," the woman on the line told her. "Whose birthday?"

"My friend Jeannie's little girls. Their birthday party is this Saturday afternoon. They're going to be ten." Carrie's pulse sped up. Ten years had already passed. Her mind tried to take her down an unhappy memory lane, but she refused to make the trip.

"Do you want to buy clothing or books or toys?"

"I'd like to buy them all those things, but probably a book or toy."

"Good. I'm coming to town to shop later today. Why don't we meet on Brown Street at the toy store?"

"You'll shop with me?" She couldn't believe a stranger would help her like this.

"Of course. If you want me to. And we'll make that big lug of a son of mine come along. He's got some birthday shopping to do himself. For his brother's daughter. Tell him I said so."

Carrie hung up, then repeated to Mike what his mother had said. Most people might not be able to picture this big man buying birthday gifts for his brother's little girl, but she knew him by now. Mike had a good heart, hidden within a forbidding exterior.

Rising, Mike greeted a customer coming in the door. He couldn't shake his reaction to Carrie's worried expression. He wished he could help her to be happier. Not only was she excellent at her job, but she also had such a sweet way with people . . . and with his Greta. You could tell a lot about a person when you saw her with a pet.

Carrie had let Mike persuade her to ride on the back of his Harley to Imaginivity, a shop unlike any toy store she'd ever seen. She gazed at the walls, lined with shelves of brightly colored boxes. Mike's mother stood beside her, slim, petite and with a face decorated with laugh crinkles around her eyes. Carrie liked Kerry Ann at first sight.

"So, Mom, we're shopping for Pete's girl?" Mike's voice rumbled.

Carrie had grown to love his deep voice. The hair on her nape prickled with awareness of him. At first, she'd been wary because of bad past experiences with men. Now she felt Mike had a cuddly quality others might overlook.

"I really like this store," Carrie said.

Mike rubbed his hands together. "Let's get shopping."

Soon the three of them carried shopping bags bursting with gifts for three little girls. Mike and Carrie halted at the curb. The motorcycle had only saddlebags. They couldn't squeeze wrapped gifts into them.

Kerry Ann snatched the bags from their hands. "Mike, let Carrie follow you out to the farm for supper." She started toward the car parked next to the motorcycle. "Greta's invited, too."

Mike gazed at Carrie. "Free for supper?"

"I don't want to put your mom out. I can just pick up my bag—"

"Now *that* would put my mom out. She wants us to come for supper. I'll take you to your car, and you can follow me out to the house." He mounted the bike and slid on his helmet.

After a brief hesitation, she did the same. She liked the solid feel of leaning into his broad back and wrapping her arms around his waist.

At suppertime, Carrie drove behind Mike up a gravel lane to his family's farm. Greta sat in the passenger seat beside her. Carrie instantly loved the large old oaks that shaded the white farmhouse and red barn. A large, obviously handmade play set entertained three children in the yard. Carrie pulled up beside Mike and climbed out of the car.

"My nieces and nephew," Mike said, motioning toward the play set.

She stepped beside him, enjoying his nearness. "Jeannie's twins . . . would love this."

"They've been here more than once," Kerry Ann called out. "Come on. You two can set the table."

Carrie and her sister had only had each other growing up.

Now watching this large family gather for a meal at a picnic table under the shady oaks was like stepping into a Hallmark movie. Joining them, she accepted a full plate.

"I've never tasted green beans like this," she murmured to Kerry Ann.

"My own recipe. Tart and Cheesy Green Beans. The beans are fresh from my garden."

"I like them the way my mom used to make them with more bacon," Mike's dad grumbled.

In contrast to Mike, he was wiry and thin and scowled as often as his wife smiled.

"That's your second helping," Kerry Ann pointed out with a grin.

"Humph," her husband replied.

"My parents are kind of yin and yang," Mike whispered in her ear. "Mrs. Sunshine and Mr. Gloom."

Carrie chuckled behind her hand.

Too soon she was inside helping Kerry Ann fill the dishwasher. Carrie felt welcome here — except with Mike's dad. He kept looking at her and then looking away. It made her nerves jump.

"Don't let my husband bother you," Kerry Ann said. "At first, he gives everybody the once over. Three or four times."

Carrie smiled back, though she was still unsettled.

After they finished in the kitchen, Carrie stepped outside, looking for Mike to say goodbye.

"What do you know about this girl?" Mike's dad asked nearby but not in sight.

Carrie's face heated. No one in town knew more about her than what she'd decided to reveal.

"She's a nice person, and she does good work," Mike replied.

"But what do you *know* about her?"

"Dad, what's your point?"

"I see that you're interested in her. She's not from around here. What do we know about her? About her family?"

Breath caught in Carrie's throat. Mike was interested in her?

"Dad, she works for me. That's all you need to know for now."

Around the bump-out of the chimney, Mike came into sight, and Carrie had no place to hide. He walked straight to her. "Let's talk."

He led her to the play set where an adult-size swing hung. Across the yard, Greta sauntered out of the shade to watch them.

"Hop on," Mike invited.

She glanced over her shoulder at him, then settled into the swing. "I haven't done this for a long time," she said, wondering what he would say.

"You shouldn't take what my dad says too seriously." He stepped behind her and pushed her swing. "He resists anything or anyone new."

The moment for truth had come. She had better set Mike straight, even if it cost her the job she loved, working with a man she now admitted she had feelings for. "Mike, I've done things I'm not proud of."

"Who hasn't?"

She drew in air and pumped her legs to keep swinging. "Have you been in prison on drug charges?" Saying these words made her feel sick.

"No. I've been in jail though."

"You have?" She twisted on the swing to view his face.

"Yeah. I ran with a rough crowd in high school and after. When I look back, I wonder why." He pushed the swing again. "I guess it's just being rebellious and not thinking about the consequences. I always thought Dad was harder on me than on my squeaky-clean older brother."

"I guess we're alike, Mike. Can I tell you another secret?"

"If you want to. It will stay with me, just like the first."

She took a deep breath and released the truth she'd held inside for so long. "My friend, Jeannie, is really my sister. Her twins are . . . mine." Now she waited. His response to *this* revelation really mattered.

Mike didn't stop pushing the swing. "That must be hard."

8

"It is. But when they were born, I couldn't take care of them. I did the right thing, leaving them with Jeannie. When they're older, we'll tell them who I really am." She choked up.

He stopped pushing the swing and stepped in front of her. "That's a good decision."

Then he did something she hadn't expected but now realized she'd hoped for. He drew her up by her hand and kissed her lips lightly. Greta gave a little yip of approval.

"At work we'll keep it all business," he murmured against her cheek, "but after work, I'd like to get to know you, Carrie."

One tiny tear slipped from her eye. "I'd like that too, Mike."

With joy, she realized that coming to live in the Northwoods had been the best decision she'd ever made. And her sister was right. Second chances in the Northwoods did happen.

A NOTE FROM LYN

I love this recipe because it blends three kinds of dairy (Wisconsin is America's Dairy Land!) with green beans and bacon. Yum! If you'd like a PDF booklet of Old Family Recipes & their stories from 15 Love Inspired Historical authors, visit my web site www.LynCote.com and subscribe to my email newsletter.

LYN'S TART AND CHEESY GREEN BEANS

2 tablespoons margarine or butter
2 tablespoons flour
1 teaspoon onion flakes or ¼ onion, chopped
1 teaspoon salt
Pepper to taste
½ cup plain yogurt or sour cream
2/3 cup cottage cheese or ricotta
3 cups fresh green beans, cooked/drained
½ cup cheddar cheese, grated
1 cup breadcrumbs
2 slices crisp bacon

Melt butter. Stir in flour, salt, onion, pepper, yogurt (or sour cream) and cottage cheese (or ricotta). Mix well. Heat to bubbling. Stir in green beans and ½ cup breadcrumbs. Pour into sprayed casserole dish. Sprinkle on the rest of the breadcrumbs and cheddar. Crumble bacon over top. Bake in 350-degree oven for 20 minutes. Serves 4.

ABOUT LYN

Author of more than 40 books, award-winning Wisconsin author **LYN COTE** writes contemporary and historical romance. Her popular "New Friends Street" series, where the characters in this story were first introduced, includes titles *Shelter of Hope, Daddy in the Making* and *Building a Family.* Visit her web site www.LynCote.com, which features the home-page blog, "Strong Women, Brave Stories," and find her on Facebook, Goodreads and Twitter.

CHANGING HER MIND

BY TERRI REED

June

Beth Thompson breathed in the clean Portland, Oregon, air as she made her way from the parking lot to the large brick building where she would start her new job. She'd grown up in the Pacific Northwest, though farther north in Seattle. Being inland felt different.

A summer drizzle moistened the air, not the same salty mist she was used to, but a lush dampness that chilled her skin and wreaked havoc with her makeup and frizzed her red hair.

So not the way she'd envisioned her first day of work.

She pushed opened the employee door of the Pacific Savings and Loan and quickly ducked inside. Warmth immediately enveloped her, chasing away the cold.

"Well, hello there." A deep baritone voice wrapped around her, adding to her sense of comfort.

She whipped her gaze toward the row of lockers against the wall. A tall, good-looking guy, wearing black slacks and a bright-green button-down shirt, smiled at her. He had the most stunning gold-colored eyes she'd ever seen. His blond hair had been swept back off his high forehead, emphasizing the angles and planes of his handsome face. Little flutters of attraction took flight in her tummy.

She gauged his age to be close to her own.

He arched an eyebrow.

Her face flamed. She was staring, and he was waiting for her to acknowledge him. "Uh, hello."

"You're the new hire. Dan mentioned there was new blood coming on board, but he hadn't said anything about how pretty you are. But then again, he's married. I'm not." He stuck out his hand. "Paul DeBarge."

Great. He . . . was flirting with her. Inwardly, she groaned. She'd transferred out of the last branch of Pacific S & L because her boss had made her life miserable when she wouldn't go out with him. She squared her shoulders, deciding she'd nip this in the bud, despite his attractiveness.

Hoping to be professional, she slid her hand into his and then, as heat shot up her arm, nearly forgot what she was about to say. This was not good. She cleared her throat. "I'm Beth. And I don't believe workplace romances work out."

Uh, had she really just say that out loud? Now he would think she was rude. Way to make a good impression. Not.

His eyes twinkled. "Good to know." He continued to hold onto her hand. "I guess you and me, dinner and a movie, is out?"

"Yes." Though for some reason, a sense of loss pricked her. She shook it off. "Is that going to be a problem?" Better to know now.

He grinned. "Not for me."

Somehow his words didn't inspire the confidence she'd hoped for. Did the guy think he was irresistible? She'd had her fill of egomaniacs.

"Come on," Paul said with a sweep of his arm toward the door leading into the bank. "I'll introduce you to the rest of the gang and show you where you'll be stationed."

August

"Here, let me help you with that."

Beth glanced up from her workstation to see Paul rush out from behind the teller partition to assist a woman, who was struggling to get a large stroller through the bank's front door. This wasn't the time first in the past two months that Paul had gone out of his way to offer aid or support to customers . . . or to her.

Just last week when she'd gone out to her car to leave for the day, she'd discovered that her tire was flat. He'd insisted on changing the tire for the spare. And he'd expected nothing in return. Which only made him more appealing. She had to admit his charm was hard to resist.

Maeve Maddsen, her work friend, nudged her elbow into Beth's rib. "That young man will make a very a good husband for some blessed woman one day."

Slanting a sideways look at Maeve, Beth refrained from commenting. It was clear her coworker wanted to play matchmaker. Well, she wasn't taking the bait.

September

Paul grew warm on this bright, sunny, fall day as he waited outside the church, hoping Beth would take him up on his invitation to join him for this morning's service. When he'd learned that they shared the same faith, he'd casually invited her, making sure it didn't sound anything like a date. He disagreed with her belief that workplace romances didn't work out. His mom and dad had met when they'd both worked in the same law practice.

The church's organ began the first hymn, and still no Beth. Disappointment filled him. He shouldn't have been surprised. For the past three months, she'd declined to fraternize with anyone outside of work. He turned to go inside.

"Paul!"

His breath hitched, and he whirled to find Beth hurrying from the parking lot. Her sundress swirled around her shapely calves, and her red hair was captured at her nape, emphasizing her slender neck. Her smile lit up her whole face.

Breathless, she came to a stop beside him. "Sorry I'm late. There was so much traffic."

Pleasure spread through his chest. He extended his arm. "No worries. You haven't missed anything."

Slipping her arm through his, he escorted her inside. He shared a look with his sister, who grinned.

His family was thrilled that he'd invited his coworker to church, despite his telling them they were only friends. He secretly wished they were more.

October

The sound of a basketball rhythmically bouncing on the hardwood floor echoed through the gym. Sweat dripped down Paul's back as he jogged down the court, the rough texture of the ball against his hand empowering him as he headed for the basket. A flash of red hair in the bleachers caught his attention. He glanced over. Beth sat in there, watching the bank employees' pickup game. He couldn't believe she'd shown up. Man, she was pretty. The flowered sweater she wore made the color of green in her eyes pop.

And she was watching him.

A thrill raced a zigzag course over his flesh, spurring the need to show off and making him press harder toward the basket. He still held out hope that she'd go on a date with him. Beth was genuine and kind, and she laughed at his jokes. After she'd put him in his place that first day, they'd struck up an easy friendship, based on professional courtesy and mutual respect. At least, he sure respected her.

For the past five months, she'd impressed him with her gentle nature and her honesty. There were no pretenses. He appreciated that. After the debacle with his last girlfriend, who'd not only lied to him but also had stolen from him, Beth was a breath of fresh air.

He whipped his gaze to the hoop, preparing for a layup. Close now. He had to make a basket. He couldn't let Beth see him fail. Taking off on his forward leg, he thrust his arms up.

The basketball rolled to his shooting hand. Paul sent the ball up, and he came down, landing awkwardly on his right foot, his ankle rolling. As pain shot up his leg and he went down hard on the gym floor, the ball swooshed through the hoop.

The collective gasp from the other players and the few spectators sounded as loud as a gunshot blast inside his head. He grabbed his throbbing ankle and bit back a howl of agony.

Fantastic. So much for impressing the new girl at the bank.

"That was horrible," Maeve exclaimed from her teller window on Monday morning. "I can't believe Paul hurt himself so badly."

Beth glanced at the older woman for a second and then went back to counting her till – and the minutes until the branch opened for business. They stood in their respective teller windows. Outside, the rain beat against the windowpanes, typical for late fall in Oregon.

"Poor Paul," Maeve continued. "Dan said he's stuck at home for a few days. He tore all sorts of stuff in his ankle. I'll bet he's bored and could use some company."

Beth shook her head at Maeve's continued attempt at matchmaking. She'd already allowed Maeve to talk her into joining her at the community center to watch the guys from the local savings and loan branches during their weekly pickup basketball games.

The memory of Paul twisting his ankle played in her mind, making her cringe. He'd been doing so well until he landed wrong. "I feel so bad for him."

The older woman nodded in agreement.

Beth glanced at Paul's empty station next to her. Work wasn't the same without him. She enjoyed his sense of humor and his work ethic. He was always punctual and generous with his time. He'd even invited her to his church and introduced her to his friends and family. Though it had been a bit awkward, she'd enjoyed both the church service and meeting the people in his life.

She'd attended another service at the church yesterday, only he hadn't been there to greet her. She missed that. And missed having him stand next to her.

Beth thought back to that first day when he'd flirted with her, playfully suggesting dinner and a movie. A part of her wished she hadn't been so quick to put him off, even though she didn't believe dating and working together was a good idea.

Maybe she was wrong. Maybe.

She couldn't deny she was tired of living in the past, tired of being lonely. She sighed. The days would be long without him working next to her. Paul was different. He was a good guy. Too good to let get away. She wished there was something she could do for him.

The first customers of the day filed in the now-open door, bringing with them the fresh scent of rain and pine.

"Here we go," Maeve murmured and then smiled at the man stepping up to her window.

Beth turned her attention to her job. For the rest of the day, as she helped customers with their banking needs, she had Paul in the back of her mind. By the time she was ready to pack up and go home, she had an idea of a way she could do something nice for Paul.

After a hurried grocery-store trip, she returned to her studio apartment in downtown Portland and went to work on making her friend a feel-better meal.

Paul stared at the television as he'd been doing since coming home from the urgent care center on Saturday. His mom had stopped by twice already with groceries and to do his laundry. He'd had to remind her that he was twenty-eight and could take care of himself. Though the laundry part . . . he was okay with her helping with that because he was still struggling to get around, while wearing a boot on his ankle and using the crutches the doctors had given him.

A knock sounded at the door. He let out a sigh. What had Mom decided he needed now?

Using his good leg, he heaved himself out of the chair, positioned the crutches beneath his arms and hobbled to the door.

As he opened it, he said, "What did you forget this time?"

His mouth dropped open. Instead of his mom, Beth stood there. His heart did a little flip.

She wore loose-fitting silky pants and an emerald-colored top that showed off the depths of color in her eyes and complemented the mane of red curls that spilled around her shoulders. His temperature shot up a notch like it did every morning when he stood next to her at the bank.

"I don't think I forgot anything," she said with a shy smile. She held a Crock-pot in her arms and had a large shopping bag slung over her shoulder. "May I come in?"

He swallowed his surprise and hopped backward. "Sure. What is this?"

"Dinner." She went to his kitchen to unload and turned to face him. "I hope you like Tomato Basil soup, salad and a fruit tart for dessert."

Giddy happiness swept through him. "I do. Thank you. That's so thoughtful of you."

A blush pinkened her cheeks. "Well, I figured this was as good a way as any to ask you to dinner." She held a DVD. "And a movie."

Delighted by the implication in her words, he hobbled over to take her hand. "What happened to not dating coworkers?"

She gave him a sheepish grin. "I've changed my mind, if that's okay?"

He brought her knuckles to his lips, which required balancing on his good leg and one crutch. "My mom always says it's a lady's prerogative to change her mind."

A NOTE FROM TERRI

Tomato Basil Soup is my personal favorite comfort food. That and grilled-cheese sandwiches. Several years ago, some women at my church formed a Gourmet Dinner Club. There were twenty-eight of us. We broke up into groups and prepared and served a meal for the whole group. This recipe for Tomato Basil Soup came out of that club. I have no idea where it originated from, but I've made it numerous times over the years for potlucks and school events. It's always a hit. I usually double this recipe and use brown sugar rather than white sugar, but that is, of course, a taste preference. I've found that the brown sugar adds a hint of caramel. I've also added garlic cloves to make a more savory soup.

TOMATO BASIL SOUP

3 tablespoons butter
1 large onion, sliced
1 large carrot, peeled and chopped
4 ripe tomatoes (any variety)
½ cup lightly packed, chopped fresh basil
¾ teaspoon sugar
1/8 teaspoon ground white pepper *
1 ¾ cup chicken broth
Salt to taste
Fresh lemon, thinly sliced
Extra fresh basil leaves

In 3-quart saucepan, melt butter over medium heat. Add onion and carrot. Cool until onion is transparent, stirring frequently. Stir in tomatoes, basil, sugar and white pepper. Heat to boiling, stirring constantly. Reduce heat. Simmer covered for 10 minutes. Cool slightly. Pour into food processor or blender and puree until smooth. Return to pan. Stir in broth and salt. Heat until steaming. Ladle into individual bowls and float a slice of lemon topped with a basil leaf in each bowl. Serves 6 to 8.

ABOUT TERRI

Award winning, multi-published author **TERRI REED** writes novels that have appeared on Publisher's Weekly Top 25 and Nielsen's Bookscan Top 100 and have been featured in *USA Today*, *Christian Fiction Magazine* and *Romantic Times Magazine*. A past finalist in the Romance Writers of America's RITA contest, Terri resides in the Pacific Northwest with her college-sweetheart husband and two wonderful children. To learn more about Terri, visit her Amazon author page.

NEW YEAR'S DATE

BY RENEE RYAN

Like it or not, Faith O'Malley had a job to do, and she was nothing if not a consummate professional. With a mixture of horror and absorbed detachment, she lifted the pea-green, one-piece, granny-style bathing suit that her program director had left on her desk at the radio station the day before. It was even uglier in the blinding beach light.

Suddenly, she needed an Advil.

This was perfect. Just perfect. Chloe had gone out of her way to embarrass her . . . again.

Point: Chloe.

Clenching the bathing suit in her fist, Faith sank into the pink plastic chair outside her beloved beach cottage on Tybee Island and took a look at the outdoor thermometer. Fifty degrees. Fifty *stinkin'* degrees.

Okay, so it wasn't too terribly cold for January in southern-coastal Georgia, but the water temperature would be unbearable at this early hour, even if she took the "plunge" in this hideous, oversized, sorry excuse for a bathing suit.

Coupled with this garment, Chloe's latest suggestion for an on-air stunt was another example of why nobody took Faith seriously around the radio station. It was bad enough that after one look at her artfully styled hair, hourglass figure and manicured nails, they instantly deemed her a walking cliché — of the all-looks-no-brains variety. Add to the mix this ridiculous participation in the annual Tybee Polar Plunge, and no one would ever look beyond the surface.

At this rate, Faith was destined to spend eternity on the morning show at WMRK. She might as well kiss her dream of serious talk radio good-bye. All right, yes, she was the owner's daughter. And that little factoid played a large part in Chloe's passive-aggressive attempts at humiliating her. But hadn't Faith earned respect over the last year on her own merit? Along with her co-host, she'd turned the *Faith and Dave Show* into the top-rated program in Savannah among women ages twenty-five to fifty-four. That was the most important demographic to snag big-advertiser interest for the radio station.

Yet, instead of discussing the latest presidential candidate's position on national defense, she was stuck performing another outrageous bit cooked up by the station's program director – aka Faith's nemesis. And this one required her to become part polar bear, part laughingstock, by jumping in the Atlantic Ocean on the first day of the New Year.

She drew in a slow, steady breath, but the scent of salt air and sand did nothing to calm her irritation. Lifting the shapeless bathing suit, she sighed again. Did Chloe really think listeners would care what Faith wore when she jumped into the frigid ocean with hundreds of other insane people? Of course she did. That was why this little stunt of hers was just plain mean.

Faith considered her options. She could feign illness. Going with it, she tested out a cough. No good. She sounded way too healthy. Or she could simply blow off the event. Maybe claim Chloe had given her the wrong time.

Except . . .

That was beneath her. Besides, today wasn't about her ongoing feud with the radio station's PD. Faith had loyal listeners depending on her to bring some level of dignity to the bits her radio show provided for their listening entertainment.

"You will not win this round, Chloe Wesson."

With time running out, Faith rushed inside the cottage and changed into the ugly bathing suit. At the last moment, genius struck. She pulled a stylish cover-up over her head before slamming out the back door. The garment was made of black mesh so tightly woven that only the barest hint of puke green showed through the holes.

Point: Faith.

Always punctual, she arrived at the Tybee Beach Pier at the prearranged time, her casserole in tow. Her Easy Cold Corn Salad was legendary around the radio station, and it would be a perfect accompaniment to the hotdogs and hamburgers the staff would share later in the afternoon for their own New Year's Day celebration.

After a cursory look around, she located the station's van parked near the entrance to the pier. Faith jogged over, the sand and tar squeaking beneath her sneakers. With years of practice, she managed to avoid cables and people alike. It looked like a good turnout, with a crowd of onlookers already gathering on the beach for the on-air stunt. Faith may have been on the radio, but with Internet streaming and weeks of promotion, their loyal listeners would get front-row seats to her humiliation.

Chloe was waiting with a scowl on her face. The moment she caught sight of Faith's getup, she rolled her eyes. "You can't be serious."

Faith blessed her with a sweet smile, innocence personified. "What? I wore the bathing suit you chose, exactly as you requested."

Before Chloe could respond, Faith's co-host, Dave, sauntered over and bumped hips with her.

"Ready to take the Plunge?" He shivered in mock fear.

Faith glanced at his jeans, sweater and tennis shoes. "No. Oh, no, no, no. Do not tell me I'm the only one getting in the water."

Dave regarded her with deceptively bland eyes, giving the impression he actually felt sorry for her, but he didn't answer her question.

Chloe did. "You're the only one getting in the water."

Point: Chloe.

As if she was keeping score right along with Faith, Chloe wore a self-satisfied smile as she handed the microphone to Dave. "*Tick-tock*. The listeners are waiting."

At the sound of that superior tone, Faith's mood flirted along the crest of a bad attitude. Chloe had set her up. Did she have "sucker" stamped on our forehead?

No, just "boss's daughter." Which was so, so, so very much worse.

"Come on, Faith, you can't bail on us now." Dave's tongue rolled over her name in a mock Southern drawl. "We've been teasing this event since the holidays began."

Despite her hostility toward Chloe, and that Dave was right, Faith had made a promise to the Tybee Chamber of Commerce. She never broke a promise. Never. She would do this live remote, not only to promote the annual polar bear plunge, but also the island itself.

Attempting to settle her nerves, she shut her eyes and released a long, slow breath. "Fine." Resignation scratched at her like little rat claws. "Let's do this."

Dave slapped her on the back. "That's my girl."

Moving as a unit, Dave and Faith stepped to the other side of the van where their team had already set out a tent and table with WMRK swag, including the fifty T-shirts they would give away throughout the day. Dave would handle most of the on-air work, while Faith joined hundreds of crazy people ringing in the New Year by diving headfirst into the frigid Atlantic.

Frigid being the operative word.

Her stomach performed an Olympic-quality, double-back somersault. She willed herself to take a breath, just a single breath, but her lungs refused to cooperate.

Dave pulled the microphone close to his mouth. "Five

26

minutes to launch. Any last words before you dive in, Faith?"

She mumbled something snarky before joining the queue of bathing-suit-clad crazies lining up at the water's edge. The moment her toe touched the water, she sucked in a hard breath and glanced back at the WMRK van. Dave gave her two big thumbs up. Committed now, she raised her hands in the air, got a good running start and launched herself into the water.

The first stab of pain was the worst, or so she tried to convince herself. She lost that argument when a wave crashed over her head. Her heart stuttered. Gasping for air, she swallowed a mouthful of saltwater. She must have committed a grave sin somewhere in her past. That was the only thing that could explain this vicious trip into agony and humiliation.

A low-flying seagull sliced through the air, swooping dangerously close. In the next instant, she felt a jolt of unspeakable pain at the back of her head. A scream followed. Hers? Or someone else's? Watery images filled her vision. And then . . .

Everything went black.

She woke to the feel of strong arms setting her on the cold sand. Someone called her name over and over and over again, but she couldn't identify the voice. Her head felt like a hammer was pounding away from the inside out.

She'd died. Nothing else made sense. But surely, death didn't come with this much pain.

"Open your eyes, babe."

Resigned to her torment, she attempted a squint. No good. No good. Too much light. She slammed her eyelids shut.

"Come on, you can do it." A smooth, masculine baritone drawled out the words in slow, easy syllables. Oh. What. A. Voice. "Look at me, Faith."

He knew her name?

Even more important, did his face match that sensual voice? Inch by painful inch, she peeled open one eye, then the other, and finally trained her gaze on the owner of that *a . . . maaa . . . zing* voice.

Her stomach tightened. The sensation was not altogether

awful, and the hunky sight before her was as far from awful as she could get. Military-short black hair, piercing green eyes, jaw speckled with day-old beard, that face belonged on the cover of a men's magazine, selling rugged outdoor gear.

Surprised by her strong physical reaction to a stranger, she ordered her chaotic thoughts under control. "What . . . uh, happened?"

His lips curved into a grin, the gesture enhancing his extraordinary looks. "A seagull dive-bombed you."

"A . . . what . . . did . . . what?"

Dave's head moved into her line of vision. "Yeah, no kidding, Faith. A seagull tried to take you out. The little bugger would have succeeded if it hadn't been for this guy." Dave indicated magazine-dude with a jerk of his head. "He ran into the water and pulled you to safety."

Faith groaned. The humiliations just kept piling on. The handsome stranger with the rockin' voice had rescued her from certain drowning. Not the most promising beginning.

Dave continued, his lips twitching now. "The best part, the very best part? The local TV station got the entire incident on tape. You're going to be the lead-off story on the noon news and maybe the six o'clock news, too."

"Tell me you're joking."

That earned her a dry chuckle from her rescuer, even as his gaze held a serious light. "Let's see if you can stand."

"I'd rather not right now." She shut her eyes and stifled another groan. At least she'd had the forethought to cover up the ugly bathing suit, or this entire incident would have been more embarrassing. "Just leave me here to die, please."

"Not a chance. Now that I've found you, I'm not letting you get away that easily. But first, let's have a look at your head." His fingers began softly probing through her hair.

"Do you know what you're doing?" Dave asked.

"I'm a doctor."

Seriously? She'd been taken out by a seagull in front of a medical professional? She didn't know whether to laugh or cringe.

28

"All right, Faith, tell me if this hurts." His hands moved gently over her scalp, then across her forehead.

The shiver that worked its way up her spine had nothing to do with pain. "I think I'm good."

Minus, of course, that large dose of humiliation.

"Okay, looks like the wound is superficial. Let's get you on your feet."

He helped her stand. Oh, boy, he was just as good-looking from a vertical angle, with the bonus of superior height and broad shoulders to add to the already handsome face.

"Does this qualify as a reason to go home?" she asked her co-host.

"That's not a bad idea," her hero interjected before Dave could respond. "But first, you need sustenance, and I'm the man who's going to make sure you get it." He leaned over her and added, "If you didn't catch that, I'm asking you out to lunch."

Wow, how could she not be charmed?

"Come on." He offered her his hand. "No more lollygagging."

With his assistance, she managed to walk back to the radio's van. A bit wobbly, she leaned on him for support, whereby she discovered he was made of solid, ripped muscle under all those wet clothes and big broad shoulders.

One step, two, and then her knees buckled. He scooped her up in his arms. Wow, oh wow, the guy had some serious moves.

"So, I," she paused, snuggling against him, "didn't get your name."

"It's Mike. Mike Wesson."

"Wesson?" What were the odds? "Any relation to Chloe?"

"Yep." He smiled down at her. "She's my sister. And you never answered my question. Are we on for lunch?"

It wouldn't be a good idea to date Chloe's brother. He wasn't precisely off-limits, but he wasn't exactly in the green-light lane, either. Why did Mike have to be related to her nemesis? Faith really wanted to go out with him.

"Well?" he prompted.

Those amazing eyes bore right through all her wise excuses. It was just lunch, she told herself. Sure, Chloe would be incensed. But what if Mike was *the one*?

"No, I couldn't." Even she could hear the disappointment in her voice. "Your sister and I aren't on the best of terms. In fact, she can hardly stand me."

He threw his head back and laughed. "That's a ringing endorsement if ever I heard one."

Huh? "Did you not hear me? I said your sister hates me."

"Excellent. It's a running joke in our family. Chloe is the worst judge of character. I think I'll ask you to marry me right now."

Faith laughed. "Let's start with lunch."

"You're on."

Game, Set, Match: Faith.

A NOTE FROM RENEE

I love this recipe for its simplicity. There's very little prep time, and it can be made several days in advance of any event or party. This dish is a hit at any family gathering, especially with the kids.

RENEE'S EASY COLD CORN SALAD

2 cans whole kernel sweet corn
1 can Shoepeg corn or white corn
½ cup red onion, chopped (optional)
½ cup red and green peppers, chopped
1 cup shredded cheddar cheese
1 cup mayonnaise
1 to 2 cups chili cheese Fritos corn chips, slightly crushed

Mix corn, onions, peppers, cheese and mayonnaise together in a large serving bowl. Refrigerate. Add Fritos just before serving so they stay crunchy.

ABOUT RENEE

RENEE RYAN is a multi-published, award-winning author, best known for her fast-paced, character-driven romances. She sold her first book by winning the inaugural Dorchester/Romantic Times New Historical Voice Contest. She currently writes contemporary and historical Inspirational Romances for Harlequin Love Inspired. An empty nester, Renee lives in Nebraska with her husband and a large, fluffy cat many have mistaken for a small bear. Find out more about Renee at www.reneeryan.com.

WHITE SOUP

BY CAMY TANG

"... as for the ball, it is quite a settled thing; and as soon as Nicholls has made white soup enough, I shall send round my cards." – Mr. Bingley from *Pride and Prejudice* by Jane Austen.

"You should put it in her apron," Spenser said.

"But she's wearing it," Edward said.

"You get there early, before she starts work, to put it in her apron. Then you'll be there when she finds it." Spenser clapped him on the shoulder. "Trust me. This'll be great."

There were ground almonds *everywhere*.

Jennifer Lim froze where she stood. The blender-cover malfunction had sprayed almonds on the counter, the walls, the windows over the sink and down her bra.

It was barely seven o'clock, and her morning already had included an explosion.

"Hey Jenn. Whoa!" Her cousin, Mimi, stood in the

doorway, eyes wide. "New facial mask?"

Jenn glared at her, wiping muck from her cheeks. "The blender cover just shot off the top like a rocket. And now I'm slimed."

"Almonded." Mimi grinned. Then she sobered and grabbed a towel to help wipe the almonds off of her cousin. "I heard about this weekend. Are you all right?"

Jenn paused in trying to scoop the grit out of her bra. Part of the reason she'd been up so early this morning was that she'd had problems sleeping last night. "I'm okay, I guess."

Mimi gave her a *Who're you fooling?* look. "From what Trish and Lex told me, it was pretty scary for them when they saw you get thrown from the raft."

"I should know better than to listen to Lex." Jenn mimicked her other cousin, "'White-water rafting in October will be fun. The drought in California means the rivers are low, and it won't be dangerous.'"

It had been a minute of scrabbling in the icy water as she'd tried to escape from where she was trapped under the raft, trying to breathe. Rocks had scratched her as she was carried with the raft over the foaming water. Only when the guide had steered them into a calm section had she been able to swim out. To take a gasping breath.

Jenn shivered, frozen by the water all around her, her heart bubbling in panic. Then suddenly she was back in her kitchen at her restaurant, Pookie's, in the Castillo Bed and Breakfast.

"Jenn—"

"I'm fine." Jenn kicked off her shoes and climbed up on the counter to wipe the almonds off the walls and ceiling.

What bothered her even more than her frightening moment had been the reaction of her boyfriend, Edward, who'd been in the raft in the raft. He'd been glad she was okay, but he'd also been strangely aloof ever since.

"What are the almonds for?" Mimi cleaned the counter after Jenn had jumped down and slipped back into her shoes.

"I'm developing some dishes for a wedding at the winery in a couple of months. The bride wants a Jane Austen-themed reception."

"Smells good." Mimi sniffed at the pot of stock on the stove.

"This'll be white soup, from *Pride and Prejudice*." Jenn stirred the soup, and the aroma of thyme and basil drifted up, along with the richness of the beef and chicken stock.

They finished cleaning up, and Jenn asked Mimi to grind more almonds for the soup. No sense tempting fate twice. When the soup was simmering with the almonds, they started baking the morning rolls for the bed-and-breakfast guests.

They were surprised when the door to the dining room opened.

Edward froze in the doorway. "Uh . . . you're here early."

"You sound like that's a bad thing."

Didn't normal boyfriends do thing like knocking aside tables to bear down on the woman and kiss her senseless? Maybe she'd watched too many chick-flicks. It didn't help that Edward stood there in all his Spanish-European gorgeousness that made her want to fling aside tables to bear down on him and kiss *him* senseless. Although knowing her luck this morning, she'd probably slip on some ground almonds and slam her face into the floor at his feet.

Edward looked . . . well, sort of like he'd killed someone and was desperately trying to figure out how to hide the body.

"Why are *you* here?" Jenn asked. "I thought you were helping your aunt with the goats this morning." The Castillo Winery was also known for award-winning artisan cheeses from their goats and cows.

"Oh . . . you know . . ." he said nonchalantly, although his eyes darted around the kitchen. "Pookie's crotchety this morning. I thought it would be better to stay out of her way."

Jenn's restaurant had been named after Pookie, the goat that, in a strange way, had brought her and Edward together. However, he was acting strangely right now, almost as if . . .

As if he were going to break up with her.

She felt as if she'd been slammed into the floor, after all, but with a piano landing on top of her.

36

Would he really break up with her? He'd been distant this weekend, but before that, everything between them had seemed fine to her. What if he hadn't felt the same way?

She worked all the time at her newly opened restaurant and also served as caterer for any winery events. Edward worked hard, too, since his uncle owned the winery, and he was being trained to take over one day. They hadn't seen each other much over the past several weeks as early fall was a busy time for them both.

Was she too boring for him? She was shy, dependable Jenn. She wasn't as pretty, fearless, fun or smart as any of her cousins. She was an engineer-turned-chef with the heart of a mouse. She even sounded yawn-worthy in her head.

"Jenn?" He looked at her with concern. She hadn't even realized she'd frozen in place, and was staring at him like he'd sprouted two heads and was dancing the hula with a fake, flower lei.

"What?" That came out sharper than she intended.

He blinked and then he started looking around her kitchen again, this time stopping on the pot on the stove. "Hey, that smells good."

"It's white soup." The almonds had turned it a pale ivory color.

"Jenn, can you help me?" Mimi gestured to the dozens of custard ramekins she'd taken from the oven and had put on a large tray. "I need to move this to the fridge."

"Sure." Jenn grabbed one end of the tray while her cousin held the other as they started toward the large refrigerator. Jenn's hands shook slightly, but she couldn't tell if it was from anger or sadness or just that her psychotic side was coming out, tempting her to jump him while wielding a chef's knife. Which didn't sound like such a bad idea right now.

"We'll make one more batch of custard," Jenn said.

"Okay," Mimi said. "It shouldn't take too—Watch out!"

But it was too late. Jenn had been walking backwards while holding the pan, and she'd already bumped into Edward, stepping on his foot and making him stumble into the stove.

"Yow!"

"Are you okay?" Jenn almost dropped the pan as she twisted toward him.

Strangely, Edward looked as pale as the soup as he stared down at the pot. Jenn and Mimi put the heavy tray on the table.

"Did you burn yourself?" Jenn asked him. "I'm sorry about that."

"Oh, I'm fine." His voice sounded hollow. And he was still staring into the soup pot.

What was wrong with him? Maybe he didn't want to break up with her in front of her cousin.

"Mimi, would you start the coffee for me? Jenn tilted her head toward the dining room. It was almost eight o'clock, anyway, and guests would be coming downstairs soon.

"Sure." Mimi gave Edward a hard look, then glanced at the pot. She headed out to the dining room.

The silence in the kitchen was broken only by the bubbling of the soup. Edward glanced at her, then down at his hands, then at the soup.

"Just do it!" Jenn's voice had risen to banshee levels. "I can't stand it."

"What?"

"Just break up with me. I'm ready." She squeezed her eyes shut and braced herself.

"What are you talking about? Do *you* want to break up with me?"

Edward sounded so bewildered that she opened her eyes again. He looked pained.

"N–no."

"Well, that sounds convincing."

"I thought you were going to break up with me."

"Why would I do that?"

"I don't know. I just . . . you looked . . ." Jenn couldn't make her mouth work properly. And then she noticed that the soup had turned a putrid green color.

"My soup!" She reached for a metal spoon, but Edward

38

grabbed her wrist.

"No, you'll scratch it."

She stared at him. Her mouth was probably hanging open, too, but her brain was working too hard for her to tell it to close. "I'll scratch what?" she asked slowly.

"Um . . . " Edward scratched his head. "I kind of dropped something."

"In my soup?" The "white soup" was now the horrifying color of a swamp. Which was appropriate because she was ready to bite his head off, alligator style.

"It was an accident. I was holding it when you bumped into me and it . . ." He winced. "Fell."

"In my *soup*?" She was starting to sound like a particularly annoying GIF, but she didn't care. "What was it?"

"A box." She reached for the spoon again, but he said, "And . . . something else."

Something that would get scratched. Hadn't he mentioned that? She huffed and grabbed potholders.

She couldn't save her soup now that it looked like something a face-sucking alien would come shooting out of. Over the sink, she poured the pot into the colander. Ground almonds like green sand. A small, squarish blob that might have once been a cardboard box now colored in streaks of gray and green. She grabbed tongs to pick it up.

"It used to be green." Edward looked pained. Or maybe he was wondering if she would bash him over the head with the mystery item. "The dye must have leeched into the soup."

"Ya think? What's in it? Why were you holding it over my soup?" Her voice was a tad screechy at this point.

"There's nothing in it now. I took it out before it fell into the pot." Edward gave a long sigh, then nodded to the colander. "This is so not how I wanted this to go."

At the bottom of the colander, covered in almonds and green soup, was a diamond solitaire ring.

Jenn shrieked and dropped the box . . . right on the ring.

Edward ran cold water into the colander, pulling the ring out. Then he went down on one knee. His beautiful eyes were dark and shining, and the way they looked at her made her breathless.

"I fell hard for you the moment I saw you," he said. "I was on my Harley, passing your car. You glanced over, and I was gone. I could have stayed there forever, riding next to you, except I didn't want to get flattened by oncoming traffic."

She laughed, and it came out a bit watery.

"When you got thrown from the raft this weekend, I—" His voice caught. "I've never been so scared in my life, Jenn. I realized I had to stop being a moron and stop wasting time. I love you. Will you marry me?"

"Oh, yes."

He slipped that slimy ring on her finger, and then he rose and kissed her hard, his hands wrapping around her waist to pull her close. She wanted to drown in him. She could smell his musk, with a hint of thyme and verbena, and also almonds. Although . . . the almond smell *might* have been coming from the grit still stuck in her bra.

She distantly became aware of a whooping sound, and they came up for air to see Mimi jumping and shouting from the dining room doorway. "That is so romantic!"

"It was supposed to be so different," Edward groaned. "I came early to put the ring in your apron before you arrived, but you were here before me. So I figured I'd just pop the question. But when I was taking the ring out . . ." He lifted her hand and kissed the almond-coated finger.

"Well, it's definitely not as gross as Trish's proposal story," Jenn said. "I think hers involved octopus."

"I don't want to talk about Trish or octopus." He swooped in and kissed her again. She put her arms around his neck as the kiss deepened.

Jenn knew she was always going to love the smell of almonds.

A NOTE FROM CAMY

I love all things Jane Austen. This soup, mentioned in *Pride and Prejudice*, is rich, decadent, and delicious, perfect for Mr. Bingley's ball. The recipe is in *The London Art of Cookery and Domestic Housekeepers' Complete Assistant* by John Farley, published in 1811. However, this is the "lazy Camy" version since the original recipe was rather tedious.

MR. BINGLEY'S WHITE SOUP

1 quart beef stock
1 quart chicken stock
½ pound bacon, chopped
¼ pound rice
¼ pound blanched almonds *
 Handful minced fresh herbs **
2 anchovy fillets, minced
5 to 6 peppercorns
1 large onion, diced
2 bunches of celery, chopped
1 cup cream (or milk for lower fat version)
1 egg yolk
* May substitute 1 cup almond milk
** Basil, thyme, rosemary, oregano, in any combination

Put all ingredients in a soup pot, except for almonds, yolk and cream. Bring to boil. Simmer partially covered for 1 hour, stirring frequently to prevent rice from sticking to the bottom of the pot. Strain solids through a colander. Discard solids. Refrigerate soup 2 hours to overnight. Skim off fat. Pulse almonds in blender with 1/3 cup water until ground – like wet sand, not almond butter. Add to the soup. Bring to a boil and simmer, covered, for 15 minutes. (Alternatively, add almond milk to taste and simmer uncovered for 15 to 20 minutes.) Strain out almonds using a wire strainer. Temper egg yolk with some hot soup, adding a little at a time and whisking. Then whisk it all in the pot. Stir in cream. Serve hot with toasted bread.

ABOUT CAMY

CAMY TANG writes Christian contemporary romance and romantic suspense as Camy Tang and Regency romance as Camille Elliot. She lives in San Jose, California, with her engineer husband and rambunctious dog. Visit her web sites www.camytang.com and www.camilleelliot.com to read free short stories. Read about how Jenn and Edward, from "White Soup," first fell in love in Camy's novella, *Weddings and Wasabi*.

THE POTATO SALAD PROMISE

BY DANICA FAVORITE

Leadville, Colorado, 1881

Ellie Murphy clutched the big yellow bowl, filled with potato salad, tightly as she made her way into the Leadville Community Church. The men were coming down from the mines today, and the women of the church had put together this community dinner to celebrate. She hoped that James Hunter would be among those returning. He'd gone up to one of the mines too far out of town to come home regularly.

Women bustled around the church, putting finishing touches on the food tables lining the wall. The pews had been moved out of the sanctuary, and in their place were tables and chairs. With pretty bowls of flowers on each table, the room looked full of promise.

But would the promise she'd hoped for come to pass?

Ellie paused to let a group of men by, her heart filling with both joy and disappointment as women rushed into their arms. Joy, because how could a person not be happy at the sight of a reunion? And disappointment that James was not among the

44

men.

The bowl of potato salad felt heavy in her arms. She crossed the room, picking her way through happy couples and trying not to disturb the contents of the bowl. Too much love and care had been put into this dish to have it ruined by her carelessness. If only her palms didn't feel so sweaty, her hands so unsteady.

Some might think this was just a bowl of potato salad. But to Ellie, it was so much more.

The day he'd left, James had looked at her solemnly, brushing aside the thick dark hair that had a habit of falling in his eyes. Every detail of his intense, brown gaze remained imprinted in her memory.

"I'm not asking you to wait for me," he'd said to her. "You're free to live your life and to fall in love with someone else." He'd paused, then had taken his hat in his hands. "But if you find, around the time folks start coming back down the mountain, that there's still room in your heart for me, you make that potato salad of yours. If I don't see your dish at the church dinner, I'll know you've moved on."

Ellie had promised herself that she'd make him the biggest, best potato salad in the world for his homecoming dinner. So here she was, ready to prove her love with a delicious mixture of red potatoes, eggs and sweet onions.

Except . . . as she saw the food tables, crowded with the dishes, her heart sank. Every single bowl on the salad table contained potato salad.

Maybelle White waved her over. "Oh! You brought potato salad, too. It's been ages since you've made it, so I figured you'd be bringing something else. I made some of my own, using your recipe, of course."

Unshed tears clogged Ellie's throat. She hadn't made her potato salad since James left because she wanted it to be special for him. Who knew that her generosity in sharing her recipe would come back to bite her? As she looked down the row of almost identical salad dishes, she caught the smiles of friends who'd all gotten their recipe from her.

How on earth would James recognize that she'd done something special for him? It was like expecting him to single out one special bean in a whole pot of soup.

Ellie set her bowl on the table, wishing she'd had some kind of fancy crystal bowl to distinguish her dish from all the others. Not everyone had used her recipe, of course, but potato salad was potato salad. She should have known that other women might bring the simple dish that was a staple at church dinners.

Looking around the room, she hoped to catch a glimpse of James. If only she hadn't wasted precious minutes arranging the sliced eggs on top in a heart pattern. Now she was late in arriving, and the place was already full of people. Happy families reunited with brothers and fathers who'd spent most of the time working in the mines.

But no James.

She smoothed the sides of her dress, though the velvet was unlikely to be wrinkled. Would James like the new dress she'd made? The dark-blue velvet had been pure vanity on her part. She'd purchased it largely because the store proprietor had said it matched her eyes perfectly. James had always said he loved staring into her eyes. As for the delicate lace edging her sleeves and collar, well, her work on those pieces had been the only way she'd known to take her mind off her worries while James was away.

Would he understand just how much she'd put into this day? Over the past two-hundred-and-nine days, Ellie had carefully prepared everything to make their reunion perfect.

All that was missing was James.

She'd never felt so alone at a church gathering before. But as Ellie watched happy couples embrace, she couldn't help but think of the times she'd spent in James' arms. Precious, stolen moments. They'd shared their first kiss last Christmas under the mistletoe. He was the only man she'd ever kissed, and she'd believed in his declarations of love. Had loved him back.

So why, when he'd left for the mines, had he asked for potato salad instead of her hand in marriage?

As if to point out Ellie's miserable situation, Shirley Bates

46

squealed loudly. Ellie turned to watch Shirley run into Dan Ford's arms. Dan had proposed to Shirley before he'd left. Now the couple was reunited, and judging by the glow on Shirley's face, Dan had brought home enough money for them to marry. If only her story were so happy.

She immediately felt guilty for begrudging Shirley even a moment of happiness. It wasn't her friend's fault that James had other ideas about his homecoming. Ellie glanced at the food tables again. Plenty of people were filling their plates with the various potato salads, sharing laughter over the limited menu. She couldn't bring herself to laugh at all.

Finally, she couldn't bear it anymore. She slipped out of the room and out of the church. Tears slid down her cheeks, so she went around to the back of the building, where she could sit unnoticed and have a good cry. All she'd wanted before James left was for him to know how much she loved him. She'd hoped and prayed for a proposal, and had, instead, received a ridiculous challenge to have potato salad waiting for him.

Well, he'd have his potato salad, all right. At least twenty bowls of it. Would he know the depth of her love when her gift was presented among so many like offerings? None of it really mattered, she decided miserably, since he wasn't there to notice.

The wind picked up, and Ellie pulled her shawl tighter around her. The festivities were barely underway, and her night was already ruined.

"Why is a pretty girl like you sitting out here all alone?"

The husky timbre startled her.

"James!" She jumped up, trying to brush away her tears.

"What are those for?" He leaned forward, then wiped them away himself. "Tonight's a celebration. No time for tears."

She gestured toward the church. "Have you been in there?"

He grinned, the smile wrinkling the corners of his eyes. "I have. And I sampled some mighty fine potato salad."

"How do you know it was mine? There were twenty bowls to choose from." Ellie knew she sounded sulky, but she couldn't help herself. It didn't seem right for some other woman's potato salad to be the fulfillment of their agreement.

"I saw you walk in with it. I was in the alcove with Pastor Lassiter when you arrived."

James pulled her to him. His crisp, clean scent told her he'd stopped for a bath before coming. Ellie inhaled again, so engrossed in having him close to her that she nearly missed his next words. "But you ran out before I could get to you."

Ellie pulled back so she could see the love in his eyes.

"Of course, I had to sample some of your potato salad before following you outside," he said with a wink. "By the time we get back in there, it'll be all gone."

She smiled. "I'll make you more."

"I hope so." Then he got down on one knee. "Ellie Murphy, will you do me the honor of becoming my wife and making me all of the potato salad a man can eat?"

"Yes!"

James rose, and Ellie threw her arms around him, kissing him even though she was supposed to let him kiss her first. She'd been waiting too long for him to ask this question to wait another second—

Ellie stopped.

"Did you just make potato salad a part of your marriage proposal?" She started to pull away, but James held her close.

"I sure did."

Then he kissed her again, just a tiny peck, but enough to make her lips tingle.

"I hate potato salad. But I can't get enough of yours. I figure if you can make me love potato salad, then you must have a whole lot of love that goes into everything you do. What man wouldn't want to marry a woman like that?"

Put like that, how was she to refuse?

Still, there was something else she had to know. "Why did you make having me bring my potato salad to the dinner such a big deal? Why the test?"

James motioned toward the steps, and they sat. "I'm no fool. All those things I said before I left, they were true. You

48

could do a whole lot better than a miner like me. I can't buy you a big house or drive you around in a fancy carriage. By staying up there and not coming down all summer, I've got a little more put away for us, but it's still not going to be an easy life."

"I don't care about those things." She reached for his hand. "What matters is that we're together. The only reason there's so much love for me to give is because you've given me so much."

"You're a good woman, Ellie-love, and I'm so glad you're mine."

James bent and kissed her again. This time, it was a long, lingering kiss, one that spoke of a promise for the future they would have together.

After breaking the kiss, James stood and held out his hand. "Shall we go share the good news?"

Ellie took his hand, and together, they walked back into the church. Everyone else must have known that James was going to propose because as soon as they entered the room, the crowd burst into applause.

Friends surrounded them, murmuring their congratulations and good wishes. When the crowd finally dissipated, Ellie's stomach gave a tiny growl.

"I guess we need to get you some of that famous potato salad." He led her to the tables.

As James had predicted, Ellie's bowl was empty.

"We can have some of Maybelle's," Ellie told him with a smile. "She said she used my recipe."

They piled their plates high with Maybelle's potato salad and chose from among the dishes other church members had provided. By the time they found a place to sit, Ellie's mouth was watering.

James took a bite of the potato salad, then frowned. Ellie watched as he slowly chewed, his face screwing up in a strange expression. Once he swallowed, he grabbed his water and gulped it down.

"I'm sorry, Ellie, but that is not your potato salad."

Ellie took a bite. It tasted the same as hers. "There's nothing wrong with it."

"There's definitely something missing, I'm telling you. Your love makes all the difference."

She might have given all the ladies in the church her special recipe, but, in James' opinion at least, there was one ingredient only she had. Her love. And she'd be delighted to share it with James for the rest of their lives together.

A NOTE FROM DANICA

Like James, I'm not a big fan of potato salad. I'll eat it if I have to, but it's not my favorite. My kids like it even less. So when a member of my husband's extended family offered to teach my kids how to make "the world's best potato salad," I was a skeptic. However, we made this recipe, and I'll confess, we all loved it. My kids ask to make this potato salad a lot. The even better part of learning this recipe is that it's been passed down in the family for generations. My husband's grandmother made it, and at every family gathering, there was bound to be a bowl of Grandma Sopz's potato salad. Actually, just as in my story, whenever my husband's family got together in Leadville, the tables were often laden with several bowls of potato salad, made by different women. If Grandma Sopz's potato salad recipe can survive after all of that competition, I figure it's got to be a winner.

GRANDMA SOPZ'S POTATO SALAD

4 red potatoes, cooked until tender
½ cup chopped sweet or green onion *
4 eggs, hard-boiled, cut in cubes
2 stalks celery, chopped
1 tablespoon sweet relish

Dressing:
1 cup mayonnaise
½ teaspoon white sugar
½ teaspoon white vinegar
3 tablespoons milk **

Peel potatoes. Cut in cubes. In large bowl, mix potatoes with hard-boiled eggs, onion, celery and relish. In a separate bowl, combine remaining ingredients and mix thoroughly to make the dressing. Add the dressing to the potato mixture. Chill. To make salad look extra fancy, slice an extra hard-boiled egg and place slices on top.

Notes:

* Grandma Sopz wouldn't use the green parts of the onion, but I like them, so I use them. You may do whichever you prefer.

** Our family is dairy-free, and we use rice milk with no noticeable taste difference.

ABOUT DANICA

A self-professed crazy chicken lady, **DANICA FAVORITE** loves living a creative life. She follows her imperfect characters on the bumpy journey to Happily Ever After as they discover the lives God created them for. Oops, that spoiled the ending of all of Danica's stories. Then again, getting there is all the fun. Stay in touch with her through her web site at www.danicafavorite.com and Facebook, or follow her on Twitter.

A SATURDAY OF SURPRISES

BY JILL KEMERER

Why did Grandpa want to watch the game here? Leann Redding heaved the slow cooker onto the kitchenette counter. The retirement village where Grandpa lived had a nice clubhouse, but she preferred sprawling on the couch in his condo she when watched college football. Didn't he enjoy spending Saturdays with his only granddaughter? Leann gave her specialty, chicken enchilada soup, a quick stir, then slipped the lid back on and set the heat to low. Maybe he'd invited friends or something. She hoped she wouldn't have to make small talk with anyone.

Leann returned to the clubhouse's large gathering room. Crimson and gold leaves drifted to the ground outside the tall windows.

"Do you know where the remote is, Grandpa?" She checked the clock. Almost time for kickoff.

For the third time, her grandfather craned his neck toward the entrance. "Check the drawer under the TV."

"Are you expecting someone?" She crossed over to where

two faux-suede couches and a pair of turquoise-upholstered chairs faced a large flat-screen television. The room was spacious with high ceilings, a gas fireplace and assorted dining tables and chairs. She searched the drawers of the entertainment center and found the remote.

"Ah, here they are." Grandpa's deep voice echoed as he walked toward the group who'd just arrived. "You're looking well, Mary."

The tiny, white-haired woman swatted his shoulder. "Oh, thank you, Stan. What a good idea to get together. This is my grandson, Dylan."

Leann discreetly studied Dylan as he shook Grandpa's hand. He appeared to be around her age, in his late twenties, and he had an interesting face. Thick eyebrows framed his dark brown eyes, and a long straight nose pointed to thin lips. She turned away. Why was she looking, anyway? If five years of solving disputes as a human-resources manager hadn't killed her desire to socialize, the blind date from last month had. The guy had objected to her wearing a Detroit Tigers tee, and he'd thrown a hissy fit when she'd suggested a burger joint for dinner. She just wanted to watch today's game in peace.

"Leann, come over here." Grandpa waved her his way. "Let me introduce you to my friends."

She drifted to them. "Hi."

"Stan's told me so much about you." Mary beamed, taking Leann's hands in hers. "What a nice coincidence that you and Dylan are here so us old folks won't bore you."

A pained expression crossed the younger man's face, and he shifted from one foot to the other. Great. He didn't want to be here, either.

"It's a pleasure to meet you." She narrowed her eyes at her grandfather, who clapped his hand on the shoulder of Leonard, a man in his eighties who Leann had met in the summer. Another elderly woman with a kind smile introduced herself as Betty. After a few minutes of chit-chat, Leann said, "Excuse me, but I don't want to miss a minute of the Wolverines beating Nebraska."

"Dylan, go watch the game with her." Mary seemed overly eager to get rid of him.

He gave his grandmother a warning glare but followed Leann.

She pressed the power button on the remote. Thankfully, the game hadn't started yet. "If you have a problem with me cheering when Michigan makes a touchdown or yelling at the TV if Nebraska scores, you might want to join your grandma."

His lips twitched. "Not a Cornhusker fan?"

"I'm a Wolverine fan. Want a Coke?"

"Sure."

She marched to the kitchenette with Dylan at her heels and grabbed two Cokes from the refrigerator, handing him one.

"What if I told you I went to Michigan State?" The corner of his mouth lifted playfully.

"We're not going to get along today, are we?" She shut the fridge.

"I don't know. Do you want us to get along?" He pushed up the sleeve of his charcoal, long-sleeved T-shirt. Muscles she hadn't been prepared for came into view. *Stop staring!* She hadn't noticed a guy that way in a long, long time.

"I just want to watch the game." Leann turned and hustled back to the television, mentally kicking herself the entire way. So she felt a slight attraction to him. No big deal. She slid all the way to the far corner of one of the couches and turned up the volume.

Dylan dropped next to her with his legs splayed. Could he take up any more room? And why didn't he sit on the other couch? The opening kickoff resulted in a first down for the Wolverines. Leann relaxed a bit, but Dylan leaned toward her, his woodsy cologne alerting her senses.

"I think our grandparents are trying to set us up." He tapped his chin with his index finger.

"What?" She sat up straight. Now that he'd mentioned it, it would explain Mary's behavior.

He continued, "I take Grams to lunch every other Saturday. She always wants Applebee's. It never changes. Today she informs me we're doing a potluck. Here."

Leann's forehead wrinkled as she digested this information. Maybe Mary wanted Dylan to have a girlfriend, but Grandpa? She glanced his way. His bald head tipped back as he laughed at something Mary had said. "I don't think my grandpa has it in him."

Dylan lifted his eyebrows. "Oh, you don't think so?"

"No."

"Okay." His light tone dismissed her, and he focused on the television.

She returned her attention to the game but couldn't concentrate. Grandpa *had* invited them without telling her.

"So, why are *you* here?" The twinkle in Dylan's eyes set off a twirling sensation in her chest.

"I watch the game at Grandpa's every Saturday."

"Hmm." He managed to fill the sound with skepticism.

She shot a frown his way. "Why is it so important for you to think that my grandfather is trying to pair me up with you?"

He pointed a finger at the television. "Shh! I'm trying to watch."

Closing her eyes, she counted to three and stood, straightening her Michigan T-shirt. She strode to the table where Grandpa, Mary, Leonard and Betty chatted. Leann bent close to Grandpa's ear. "I'm going to your condo to watch the game."

He twisted to face her. "What's wrong with the TV here?"

"Nothing."

"Then stay," he said firmly and shifted to his friends.

"Are you feeling unwell, dear?" Betty's voice was as soft as her wrinkled cheeks. "Do you need a little nap?"

Leann quickly shook her head. "No, I'm fine. I get—"

"You're alone too much," Grandpa interjected.

"I wouldn't say that." She tucked her hair behind her ear as her grandfather and his friend exchanged a look. What was that all about?

He patted Leann's hand. "A pretty girl like you should be out with young people, not cooped up with her grandpa every

Saturday."

A lead weight dropped in her gut. The words "pretty girl" and "cooped up" ignited her alarms. Her grandfather really was trying to pawn her off on Dylan. As if she couldn't find a boyfriend on her own.

Her last three dates flickered through her mind. Well . . . Grandpa might have something there.

"Okay." With her chin high, she glided to the couch kitty-corner from the one where Dylan sat. Nebraska had scored a touchdown in her absence.

She ground her teeth. Lovely. Her team was losing, Grandpa was acting weird, and – she glanced at Dylan, who'd propped his legs up on the edge of his couch – this guy had made himself right at home. Fine. If she had to stay here, she was going to be comfortable, too. She stretched her legs out and rotated her neck to stare at him. "I think you might be right about them trying to set us up."

His eyes lit up as he smiled. Her breath caught. His face morphed from interesting to handsome. Just. Like. That.

"Settle in. It's not a big deal," he said. "When Grams told me there was a change of plans, I thought I'd be playing checkers with her friends. Instead, I get to watch the game."

His answer made her pause. He didn't seem to be bothered by elderly meddling. In fact, he had a pretty good attitude about the whole thing. Maybe she should go with the flow. Make an effort with him.

"Do you live around here?" She pulled a throw pillow to her chest. "I have an apartment on the other side of town."

"By the soccer fields?"

She nodded. "Yeah."

"I'm five minutes north of them. I jog or bike around the park a few times a week."

"I walk there often." Leann barely registered the announcers yelling about an interception. "Where do you work?"

"Seifert Corporation. I'm in the purchasing department."

"We work with Seifert. I'm in human resources at Delco."

A roar from the TV distracted her. "Yes! Michigan scored. Woo-hoo!" Leann jumped up and wiggled her arms and hips in a victory dance. "Go Blue!"

"What was that?" He snickered, opening his hands, palms up.

She crossed her arms over her chest. "Hey, I warned you. Things get strange when I'm watching football."

"I didn't mind." Dylan extended his arm across the back of the couch. "Do it again."

"No way." Heat climbed to her cheeks, but he started raving about the field-goal kicker.

Before she knew it, the second quarter was in full swing. Dylan told her about his clean-freak roommate, and she laughed hard, harder than she had in weeks. Maybe years.

A few minutes before the half ended, Dylan leaned forward with his elbows on his knees. "What smells so good? I'm starving."

"It's almost halftime. Let's eat." She moseyed to the kitchenette and took the chip dip, mini-turkey-sandwiches, shredded cheese and sour cream from the fridge. "Grab those bowls and plastic spoons, will you?"

Dylan opened the package of disposable bowls and set a stack of them next to the Crock-pot. "What else?"

"Tell your grandma and the others that the food is ready if they want to eat." Leann set everything on the counter while he made his way to the table. When she uncovered the soup, she closed her eyes and inhaled the spicy aroma. Perfect for a fall day.

Dylan returned. "They're not hungry yet."

She grinned. "More for us."

"Looks good." His mocha eyes captured hers. She blinked. Was he talking about the soup? Or something else?

"Yeah, well, there's a table over here where we can still see the television." They carefully carried their bowls of soup to the table, and Leann dragged a bag of chips and two more drinks over.

"Mmmm. Wow! This is delicious. You made it?" A strand

of cheese stretched from Dylan's mouth to his spoon, and he swiped it up. "I might have to come here every Saturday."

Leann didn't mind that thought at all.

Grandpa and Mary approached. Mary set her small hand on Dylan's shoulder. "Are you two enjoying yourselves?"

Leann met Dylan's gaze. Her lips twitched upward as he winked.

"Sure are, Grams."

"Good. Mary and I, well, we wanted . . ." Grandpa stared at the ground. "We have something to tell you." He put his arm around Mary. "We're dating."

Leann's soup went down the wrong way, and she sputtered, lunging for her bottle of water. Dylan's neck turned brick red, and he blinked. Repeatedly.

"We weren't sure how to tell you, so we thought maybe it would be best if we were all here together." Mary rested her short white curls against Grandpa's arm.

Leann gulped the water, unsure how to respond. Her grandfather? With a girlfriend?

"You," Dylan pointed from Mary to Stan, "are dating him? But I thought . . ."

"You thought I was too old to date? Is that it?" Mary's lips trembled, and her big blue eyes shone with uncertainty.

Leann held her breath. *Say the right thing, Dylan. Don't break her heart.*

"No, no, Grams. I'm glad you're . . . you . . . found a . . . uh, boyfriend?" Dylan's jaw went slack. "Sorry, I thought you were trying to set me up with Leann."

Grandpa bellowed with laughter. He shook his head. "Mary and I gave up hope on either of you dating anyone, let alone each other. No, we just didn't know how or when to tell you."

"I'm happy for you." Leann hugged Grandpa then Mary.

Dylan shook Grandpa's hand and kissed his grandmother's cheek. Holding hands, the older couple made their way to the kitchenette.

"So I guess you were wrong," Leann teased.

"I guess I was." He nodded. "But they were wrong, too."

"How's that?" She crumbled tortilla chips into her soup.

"About us. What do you say we watch the game at my place next week?"

Could her heart smile? Because it felt as if it had lit up. "I don't think so." She held back a grin. "Your clean freak of a roommate couldn't handle it. We'll watch the game at my apartment."

"What can I say?" He reached over and squeezed her hand. "Go Blue!"

A NOTE FROM JILL

I love this soup because it warms you up when it's cold outside. I created it after days of being stuck indoors during a brutal snowstorm. Instead of making another pot of spaghetti, I played around with the ingredients in my pantry. This soup is so easy to put together, and my whole family loves it. I hope you enjoy it, too!

JILL'S CHICKEN ENCHILADA SOUP

¼ cup chopped onion
1 tablespoon olive oil
1 tablespoon butter
3 cups chicken broth
1 cup cooked chicken
1 cup frozen corn
1 can (15-ounce) black beans, drained and rinsed
1 can (10-ounce) red enchilada sauce
1 tablespoon chili powder
½ cup milk
¼ cup half and half
½ cup shredded cheddar

In large pot, sauté onion in melted oil and butter. Add broth, chicken, corn, beans, enchilada sauce and chili powder. Cook on medium for fifteen minutes. Stir in the milk, half and half and cheese. Serve immediately. Optional: Sprinkle additional cheddar over each bowl of soup, add a large spoonful of sour cream and crumble tortilla chips on top. Serves 6.

* For a less spicy soup, add an additional cup of broth.

ABOUT JILL

JILL KEMERER writes inspirational romance novels with love, humor and faith. Her debut novel, *Small-Town Bachelor*, will be available April 2015 through Harlequin™ Love Inspired. Jill loves coffee, M&Ms, fluffy animals, magazines and her adorable mini-dachshund. She lives in Ohio with her husband and two teenagers. For more information about Jill's books, stop by her web site, www.jillkemerer.com.

HAPPILY EVER RAFTERS

BY CHERYL WYATT

"It's Christmas Eve. What in tarnation is that woman doing now?" Leavada Elliott's red polish gleamed as she swept homemade rose curtains from Grant Milan's Christmas-decorated window. He'd taken his grandmothers into his cozy home when life had left them widowed.

Turns out, he'd been the one blessed by the always wise, always listening, ever loving, creatively frugal but impeccably dressed souls.

Never mind that his bathroom now contained the biggest perfume collection known to man. His entire home smelled like Jergen's lotion and White Shoulders.

He watched his other grandma, Nellie Blankenship, humming to her Conway Twitty record, lean forward in her brown recliner. She trained her hawkeyed focus on the new neighbor's yard. "She's a fiddling with a ladder and her roof."

"Grant, come look-a here," Granny Vada whispered conspiratorially.

He loved how the two spry spies "looked out for their

neighbors" as they described gawking. In reality, the Granny Surveillance Duo neighbor-watched to entertain themselves and have something to gab about over coffee.

Wait. They'd said *roof and ladder.* Sleet was forecast today. Grant poured diced potatoes into tonight's soup and went to examine the scene outside the window.

Oh, no. "Be right back." Grant grabbed work gloves on his way out to investigate why his neighbor was hiking rooflines in Christmastime weather.

"Miss?" Grant said on approach, not wanting to scare her since she was halfway up a ladder tilted like knobby-kneed reindeer legs.

She whirled. Blinked wide. "Hello." Her cheeks grew candy-cane red when he grinned up at her. "I'm your new neighbor."

He nodded, feeling an odd sense of lightness in his chest as she smiled shyly down at him. He rested three fingers on his sternum, wondering at the feeling. Indigestion? Couldn't be. He'd skipped lunch, knowing he and his grannies were making his favorite, their infamous soup and pinched biscuits for Christmas Eve dinner, on which he would gorge.

"My name's Virginia West." She indicated the red classic Gran Torino with silver bullhorns on the hood. "And I'm stealing that car."

"You'd have a fight on your hands, considering it's my granny's, and she uses it to gallivant around, teaching my other granny how to flirt with truckers." He grinned.

She grinned back. "Nice to meet you…?"

"I'm Grant Milan. And your name is going to be on an Oklahoma hospital ER roster if you don't climb down from there," he teased.

"I keep hearing something. I've had critter problems galore. Yesterday it was bats in the rafters. Today, a snake on my concrete porch blocked my door. I chased it off with a hammer. Last week another neighbor's spider monkey, Maynard, ran off with my house keys and newest angel knickknack and made me miss the wrestling championships on

TV."

Knickknacks and wrestling? Grant grinned. His grannies would love this gal. He tuned back in to the plight she'd described.

"Now, there's a bird or squirrel or something stuck up there." She indicated the eaves.

As if on cue, scratching sounded. Then weak *mews*. "I heard that."

"Me, too."

"Here, let me try," he said. "I at least have gloves and work boots for traction."

Nodding, she allowed him to lead her down the ladder.

He admired her southwestern complexion, almond-shaped eyes and flowing long brown hair and then turned his attention to her lime-green Ford's Land of Enchantment plates.

"New Mexico, huh?"

"Yes. I was a waitress at the Dinner Bell near Bluewater Lake. But, well, life changed. Now I'm the new cook at The Monte Carlo. I start after Christmas break."

Grant repositioned the ladder and took in every word she'd said. His thoughts circled back and hinged on one phrase in particular, simply because of the pain that had lashed across her pretty eyes, Spanish like her accent.

Life changed.

Yeah. He totally knew the feeling. His thumb brushed the barren white line where his engagement ring used to be. His church's tradition of asking both men and women to wear rings to signal their commitments to wed had once seemed so sweet, but now the mark remained as a reminder of empty promises.

Her gaze followed his motions. "Looks like life changed adversely for you, too?" Spoken softly, vulnerability rushed across her caramel eyes.

There it was again. That funny feeling in his chest. Bad breakfast eggs?

Or something else?

"Recently?" She held the ladder as he climbed it.

"Ten months ago. My fiancé left me at the altar." He shrugged. "My grannies claim it's the guy who usually bolts in altar-style breakups."

Her eyes widened, then softened. Then, surprisingly, she giggled. "Your grannies know their stuff. So . . . interesting coincidence. My fiancé was a no-show at the altar, too. I hope yours at least had decency to call and let you know."

Grant donned gloves then pulled the underside guard off the eaves. "Nope. She texted my sister, Cherlise."

"Ugh! I'm so sorry. I know how it feels. My broken engagement was seven months ago, and I still struggle sometimes."

Grant grew amused at the livid look on her face. Like she was tempted to go stomp his ex. Frantic skittering sounded near his head. The mewling grew louder as he pulled another eave section off.

"Careful!" she said, as Grant plunged his arm elbow-deep into the space. After a moment, he pulled his arm out and . . . a vehemently hissing kitten.

"My goodness. It's so tiny!"

Grant smiled. "There you are."

"Are, what?" Virginia reached, but the fur ball scrambled back, panting and wide-eyed.

The kitten looked almost too weak to bite or scratch.

"The last owner left her pregnant cat. She had the kittens here. A rescuer picked up three but couldn't find the fourth and assumed she perished."

"She's been in there alone all this time?"

"Yeah, that was a week ago. No telling what she's been eating to stay alive." Grant hugged the kitten close. "Let's go get her warm, cleaned up and something to eat and drink."

"She's so cute!" Virginia gushed as she walked alongside Grant. Halfway across gravelly Richards Road that separated his yard from hers, she screeched to a halt. "Oh, wait. Sorry!"

Grant paused, cast her a questioning glance. An adorably confused look graced her face. Then it dawned on him. She probably felt awkward tagging along. He smiled at how naturally they'd fallen into step with one another.

Almost as though they were meant to.

That wispy feeling brushed through him again and this time, he knew. *Exactly.* What it was.

Hope. Fluttering its wings for the first time in a long time.

Grant nodded toward his home. "Well? What are you waiting for? We've got a kitten to care for."

Her face erupted in a grin, and she bolted forward. Past him. She reached his door and held it open as he entered. He paused on the stoop, leaned close, inhaling her sweet essence and honeysuckle perfume. "Warning, there are two spies living here."

Mirthful eyes widened. "Spies?"

"Yes. I'm pretty sure, anyway, since they perform constant surveillance on the neighborhood."

"That's okay. I saw their faces squished in the window the past few days, watching my every move. I thought they were cute."

"Cute. Right. Those two are as ornery as the hills. Another caution, they, uh, have a penchant for matchmaking. I apologize in advance if they pull any Cupid maneuvers. I'm sure they'll try, considering how beautiful you are."

Her eyes brightened. "I'm beautiful?"

He swallowed. "Yeah. That sorta slipped out."

She beamed. "By all means, let a slew more unintended compliments slip out."

He laughed, then grew serious. "I meant what I said. Though unintended, it's true."

She turned serious, too. "You have no idea how much I needed to hear that. Or . . ." Her gaze skimmed across his barren ring finger before returning to his eyes. "Perhaps you do."

He nodded, enjoying the birth of a solid and special bond.

"What shall we call her?" Virginia scratched the kitten's chin until its purrs rumbled.

"Cherlise, after my sister."

"Cherlise, it is."

Content, the kitten curled into Grant's heart and nuzzled Virginia's hand.

"Awww. She trusts you." Virginia's gaze rose to meet Grant's and seemed to say the same of her and him.

"I see that." He chuckled at the kitten, now nipping Virginia's fingers.

Nellie, armed with a bag of baby carrots and a can of corn, said, "Grant! Introduce us to your friend."

Vada, can of beans in each fist, added, "Come on in fellas. Sit a spell!"

Grant turned to find both grannies, watching from the kitchen doorway. He grinned at Virginia. "See what I mean?"

She blushed. "Did they hear everything we said?"

He smirked. "Probably."

Granny Vada, normally a dog person, yet having a heart for all animals, came and exchanged the kitten for the beans. "What we got here? This yours, young lady?"

Virginia smiled. "I'm hoping so.. I'll have to ask the landlord, but I'm pretty sure Mrs. Eroh will let me keep her."

Grant smiled as Granny Vada sang the oldies song, "Hello Walls." Phenomenal voice. And a fixer of hearts, feelings and household things.

"Mrs. Eroh's like family. She'll let you keep this cutie. She has a soft spot for critters, too. Did you find her up in the rafters with the bats?"

Virginia pointed. "I knew it! You two were eavesdropping on us."

"'Course we were. It's not every day we see Grant smile like that."

"Like what?"

"Like the moment he looked up and saw you grinning down that ladder at him." Vada tugged their sleeves. "You young'uns go finish the soup. Me and Nellie'll bathe and bottle feed this baby."

"Maybe this time next year, we'll be snuggling a real baby." Nellie wiggled eyebrows at Grant and Virginia, to whom she bestowed her carrots and corn.

"Oh." Virginia blushed. "I'd love a wedding ring before the teething ring."

"Then git your britches in that kitchen and learn that recipe. It's a surefire way to his heart."

Virginia, looking shell-shocked, followed Grant.

"Sorry about that." He chuckled and stirred broth while Virginia poured in the corn.

She peered up at him. "Are you, really? Because I'm not sorry."

He poured beans into the simmering pot. "Nice to know. So, does that mean you'd stay for dinner if I asked?"

"As long as you show me how to make this soup. I might have a man on the horizon that I'd like to impress."

"I'd say that's a win-win for us both."

After saying grace, they enjoyed a delicious, lively dinner. While Grant washed dishes, his grannies introduced Virginia to their many knickknacks. Granny had lots of silly and family-centric goodies displayed. Vada's consisted mostly of candles, pristine angels and various wall-rug collections, depicting Bible scenes.

"So sweet. Like a museum of memories," Virginia said of the knickknacks when Grant returned.

The out-of-tune quartet sang, laughed and danced along with Nellie's classic country records. They settled into the living room, sipping coffee and reflecting on Jesus, the real reason for the season, as "The Little Drummer Boy" thumped his heart out through speakers.

Sprinkled amid the merriment was kitten cuddling and shared laughter at Cherlise's playful antics. The kitten had really perked up after nourishment and a much-needed bath. After the grannies smoked Grant and Virginia at a marathon game of cards before retiring to bed, Grant settled next to Virginia on a braided throw rug beneath a wagon-wheel love seat.

"Hard to believe this is Christmas Eve. That was sweet of your grannies to invite me for Christmas dinner and teach me how to make their holiday stuffing, potato salad and chocolate gravy as well as Hoopendiker Soup and Pinched Biscuits. In turn, I taught them how to make green chili and stuffed sopapillas. I love your family, Grant."

A fleeting thought hit that she'd someday soon be part of it. He smiled. Then frowned. "It's only been seven months. Sure you're over that guy?"

"I'm sure. I only find it hard to look back on that day sometimes because rejection's painful. Yet it's tough to look ahead because I'm scared of it happening again."

"So, I have a suggestion." He took her hands in his free one since his other held the fluffy sleeping kitten. "Don't look behind or ahead. Look beside you."

She blessed him with a cheeky grin. "Why would that be?"

His smile brightened. "Because beside you is where I am, and, if I have my way, where I'll always be."

A NOTE FROM CHERYL

This soup and biscuit recipe is close to my heart because of my grandmothers, Leavada Elliott and Nellie Blankenship. They were outstanding cooks, shared everything they had and almost always had crowds at dinnertime. You could literally not leave their houses without eating. They both had the gift of hospitality in spades. I'm so thankful for the blessing of being their granddaughter and knowing them. They both impacted my life in so many good ways. Eternal ways. I love and miss them dearly and look forward to seeing them again. I'm sure that if Heaven has a kitchen, my grannies are side by side, making this meal while chatting, cackling, sipping coffee and spying on neighbors together.

GRANNY'S HOOPENDIKER SOUP & PINCHED BISCUITS

1 can of V8 juice
12 whole baby carrots
1 Vidalia onion, diced
1 can of butter beans
Handful of diced celery leaves
Salt, garlic, pepper to taste
4 potatoes, finely diced
1 pound of lean ground beef
1 can of kidney beans
1 can of corn
1 can of cooked chicken breast
Handful of angel hair pasta

Boil beef until almost done. Drain fat. Add water, onions, potatoes, carrots, salt, pepper, garlic and celery leaves. Boil until almost done. Add pasta. Boil until soft. Add corn, beans, chicken breast and V8. Slow-simmer until dinnertime. Make pinched biscuits while waiting.

Biscuits:
3 cups of self-rising flour
1 cup of milk
2 tablespoons of shortening
Pinch of salt

Sprinkle flour onto foil. Preheat oven to 375 to 400. Heat shortening in pan. Mix milk, flour and salt into a batter. Knead onto foil. Pinch off tennis ball-sized clumps of dough. Set smooth-side-down in heated oil. Flip biscuit. Set back in heated pan. Press flour into pinched portion of dough left on foil. Pinch next biscuit. Repeat process until all biscuits pinched and oiled on top and bottom. Bake 20 to 25 minutes or until golden brown. Serve with Hoopendiker Soup. Enjoy!

ABOUT CHERYL

Award-winning author **CHERYL WYATT** writes romance with virtue for the Christian market. When she's not wrangling awesome kids, spoiled Yorkies and Cute Rocker Dude, she delights in the stealth moments God gives her to write. She stays active in her church and in her laundry room. She loves readers and cherishes interaction with them on Facebook. Join her newsletter for goodies exclusive to subscribers via her web site: http://www.cherylwyatt.com.

MAIN DISHES

SCULPTURED HEARTS

BY DEBRA ULLRICK

Skylar Klein stood back, admiring the ice sculptures on the main street of Skiiridge, Colorado. It saddened her to think that all this beauty would melt when the weather turned warm. At 15 degrees, there was no chance of that happening now.

She stepped inside the ice castle, amazed at how real it looked. When she came out the other side, she admired the eight-foot grizzly ice sculpture, with its bared teeth, as well as the life-size elephant and the locomotive. Her attention snagged on an ice creation of woman's face with a faraway look and a single tear on her cheek. Skylar nibbled on her angora mitten and rummaged through all sorts of scenarios about why the artist had sculpted such a sad face.

"Skylar?"

She spun around. Her foot slipped on the hard-packed snow, but she regained her balance. Still, she couldn't believe her eyes.

"Colby?" His name rushed out in one long white puff. She

threw her arms around him, holding him, remembering how great his strong arms felt. How she'd missed him.

A good twenty seconds passed before she stepped back and drank him in with her stare. She'd never forgotten his striking gray eyes, his handsome face, his soft dark hair, his firm square jaw or his masculine lips that had once kissed her with deep passion and love. "It's so good to see you again."

"It's good to see you, too. You look great." He smiled.

Oh, how she remembered that smile. The very one that had melted her heart like ice sculptures left in the late-spring sun.

"So do you." Boy, did he ever. "What are you doing here?"

"I could ask you the same thing."

"I'm here on business." She didn't get many jobs outside California, but this one, from a new client, had been a nice opportunity.

"So am I."

"Wow, that's a coincidence."

"It sure is," he agreed.

She tilted her head. "Now what would you, a world-renowned ice sculptor, be doing here in a small ski resort town?"

Colby looked over her head.

Skylar turned and followed his gaze to the ice sculpture of the teary-eyed woman. "You did that?"

"I did."

She studied the sculpture again. "I have to know. What was going through your mind when you did this?"

He cupped his hands and blew into them. "I'll tell you, but not here. It's freezing." A puff of white accentuated his words.

"That, coming from someone who works with ice all day." She grinned.

"I don't always work with ice. It's just one of my mediums. Listen, let's go someplace warm. I'll tell you all about it, and we can catch up on old times."

"Sounds great." Her heart skipped at the idea of spending more time with the man she'd let get away.

Colby Beck offered Skylar his arm. They strolled up the street and into a local coffee shop. "You still drink hot chocolate with peppermint?"

"You remembered."

Her dimpled smile was as beautiful as he recalled as well. It lit up any room she entered.

"I remember everything."

And before he said more than he should have, Colby quickly ordered, then led her to a corner table. They removed their coats and sat down. He couldn't believe Skylar, the woman he'd never stopped loving, was with him again. Why had he ever let her get away? What a fool he'd been. Back then, they were both young and foolish, allowing their ambitions to separate them. They'd chosen their careers over their relationship. He'd moved to Colorado, and she'd stayed behind in California.

Did she regret it as much as he did?

Cupping his latte in his hands, he rested his elbows on the table. "How have you been, Skylar? And what have you been doing for the last seven years?" He already knew the answer, but he wanted to hear it from her.

"Running my catering business."

"How's that going?"

"Great." Her blue eyes brightened. "Business is booming."

"That's awesome. I'm happy for you."

"Thanks." Her dimples appeared again. "I'd ask you the same question, but the truth is, I already know."

That surprised him. "How do you know?"

"I've been following your blog all these years."

"You have?" Hope slipped into his heart. He stared into her eyes. "Why?"

"Because," she paused, glancing down at the table, "I've never forgotten you."

He reached for her hands.

She glanced at their hands, then up to his face.

"I've never forgotten you either, Skylar."

"You . . . you haven't?" Her gaze searched his.

"No." He shook his head. "I haven't."

"You never said on your blog if you ever married. Did you?"

He glanced at their clasped hands and chuckled. "If I did, I'd have a lot of explaining to do about holding another woman's hands right now. And not just any other woman's hands, but the woman I once loved."

Once. Skylar's hope was dashed with that single word. She slipped her hands out of his, hoping the beating her heart had just taken didn't show.

"So, tell me about the woman in the sculpture. Why the sad face and the big teardrop?"

Colby frowned as if he didn't understand why she hadn't responded to what he'd said. She couldn't. Saying it would rip her heart right out.

"It's a portrait of my great-grandmother."

"Really?" Skylar brushed the blond hair off her face. "Your great-grandmother?"

"Yes. For years, I heard about my great-grandfather, and how he'd left my great-grandmother and their three children with his family in Germany. How he'd come to the United States in hopes of providing a better life for them. And how it had taken years before he could save enough money to send for them.

"Shortly after they were reunited, Grandpa Great took a new job on a cargo ship. His first day on the job, Grandma Great stood on the dock, begging him not to go. She didn't feel right about it, but he assured her all would be well. His ship went down at sea, and she never saw him again."

"How awful."

"It was." His gaze connected with Skylar's. "To keep his memory alive, every year, on the eighth of June, the day his ship went down, my grandma and my mom made German piggies because that was the first thing he wanted Grandma Great to make when she arrived in the states. He loved them and missed them. So do I."

80

"What are piggies?"

"Cabbage rolls or Pigs in a Blanket. I tried to make them using my grandmother's recipe, but they didn't turn out. The cabbage wouldn't stay on. In fact, they ended up looking like something out of a horror movie. Revenge of the massacred cabbage heads."

They laughed.

"I'm curious," she said. "Why did you sculpt such an important piece of your history out of ice? Something that'll melt and vanish forever? Why not stone?"

Colby shrugged. "It's my way of letting go of the past."

Something about the way he said it and the way he looked at her had Skylar wondering if he was sending her a message. Earlier, he'd said "once loved," and now he talked about forgetting the past. Is that why he was in Skiiridge now, to put the past behind him? Including her? If he needed her to, as painful as it would be for her, she would let him go again.

She still loved him. Had never stopped loving him. That's why she followed his blog religiously. It was her way of keeping him in her life. If she could have admitted that she'd made a mistake, she would've contacted him years ago.

She didn't want to delay the inevitable, so she glanced at her watch. "As much as I hate to, I need to go. I'm catering a charity benefit for one of my clients who owns a house here."

"Darla McMillin."

It wasn't a question, which surprised her. "Yes." She frowned. "How did you know?"

"She hired me to do the centerpiece."

"Oh." Excitement pinged through her until she remembered his words. "I'll see you there then?"

"You sure will." His sparkling eyes and sly grin had her frowning and wondering what that was all about.

Three days later, Skylar hadn't seen or heard from Colby. She thought for sure she would see him before the charity dinner started. After all, he was doing the centerpiece. Speaking of the centerpiece . . . She glanced around the elegant banquet room, filled with linen-covered tables, crystal goblets and blue napkins, folded in the shapes of roses.

But no centerpiece.

Where was it? For that matter, where was Colby?

She tapped her chin, worrying and wondering if he would even show up. He had to. It would hurt his career if he didn't. Plus, she had a surprise for him.

An hour later, the room was filled with guests, but there was still no sign of Colby.

"Ladies and Gentlemen."

The voice of the hostess, Darla McMillan, snagged Skylar's attention.

"May I have your attention, please?" Darla said. "We have a special surprise this evening. Most of you, I'm sure, are familiar with the renowned ice sculptor, Colby Beck."

The crowd applauded.

"A while back, Colby came to me with a special request, and I found I just couldn't say no." Her focus shifted to Skylar. "Skylar, would you come up here please?"

Me? Skylar glanced around the room, wondering why Darla would want her to go up to the podium. Skylar's dusty-blue chiffon, V-back evening gown flowed freely as she strolled up to the hostess.

"Tonight's meal has been generously donated by Skylar's fabulous catering business, SK Gourmet Delights."

Heat rushed to Skylar's face as the crowd stood and clapped. When the applause ended and everyone was seated again, Darla looked toward the floor-to-ceiling windows that covered one whole wall of the room.

"Gentlemen, if you would pull the curtains back now, please."

The curtains slid back. There, outside the window, was a huge, magnificent ice sculpture with a lighted castle, a Cinderella carriage and two large joined hearts. In front of those hearts in the sculpture, a prince and princess leaned toward each other with their lips puckered. Up higher, as if in the heavens, was a smaller version of Colby's great-grandmother's face. Only she wasn't sad; she was smiling now and gazing down at the happy couple.

Suddenly the lights on the sculpture dimmed, and an ice ribbon with red lights appeared. It read, "Skylar, will you marry me?"

Skylar pressed her hand against her heart, searching for Colby.

"I'm right here. Behind you."

Skylar whirled.

Colby, in a black tuxedo, on bended knee, held a small silver tray with two ice-sculptured hearts and an open ring box.

"Skylar, when I said I wanted to forget the past, I wasn't speaking about my great-grandmother. I was thinking about *our* past. A past where we allowed other things to become more important than us. Yes, that sculpture will melt, but our love for each other hasn't and never will.

"I love you, Skylar. Let's not waste any more time. Grandma Great lost her love to the sea. Let's not lose ours to our careers. Please, say you'll marry me."

His eyes looked so hopeful. Tears slid down Skylar's cheek as joy flooded her heart. She rushed to him, cupped his face and kissed him.

"I love you, Colby. Always have. Yes, I'll marry you. Tonight if you'd like."

Chuckling, he stood and slipped the marquee diamond on her finger. "How about tomorrow?" He glanced around at the crowd, encouraging him with their applause. He pulled her into his arms and kissed her.

There was enough heat in his kiss that if he wasn't careful those two ice hearts would melt in a second. Which was fine with her. Like Colby said, their love had never melted away and never would.

After many congratulations, Skylar pulled Colby into the kitchen. "I have a surprise for you." She handed him a plate from the warmer.

He removed the cover, and his smile lit up the room. "Piggies!" He forked a bite. "Ummm. Every bit as good as my

83

grandmother's. What do you say we have these every year on this date?"

"I say we forget the past and focus on the future."

"I say you're right." He set the plate down, pulled her into his arms and kissed her until her knees melted like a hot ice sculpture.

A NOTE FROM DEBRA

I grew up with German piggies, (Pigs in a blanket.) I sometimes make them for our annual 4th of July party. My aunts and grandmother used to make them often – for German Dutch hop weddings and for "winching." Every New Year's Day, we'd go "winching," which is wishing my relatives a Happy New Year in German. We would say in German, "I wish you luck in the new year, long life and health and freedom amongst each other and after your death, heaven. The loving sweet Jesus we wish into your heart." At every house where we winched, there was always a huge spread of food. Piggies were one of the specialties.

MY FAMILY'S PIGGIES RECIPE

3 pounds hamburger
1 pound ground pork sausage
1 to 1 ½ cups rice
2 onions, finely chopped
2 teaspoons salt
1 teaspoon pepper
2 medium heads cabbage
1 small can sauerkraut
½ cup apple cider vinegar
3 cups water

Mix hamburger, sausage, rice, onions, salt and pepper in large bowl. Core cabbage. Either steam the whole cabbage head after coring it, or freeze the cored cabbage head a few days ahead and then thaw it at least 24 hours before using it. * Peel whole leaves off cabbage. Pinch off a handful of the meat/rice mixture and set on the edge of the cabbage leaf, roll up and tuck the ends in. Layer piggies in either a roasting pan or an electric roaster oven. Spread can of sauerkraut over the top. Mix water with apple cider vinegar. Pour over piggies. Make sure to add enough water to cover them. Regular Oven: Bake, covered at 325 degrees for 2 to 3 hours. Electric Roaster: Slow cook for 7 to 8 hours at 200 degrees to ensure that the pork is thoroughly cooked. **

* Debra found freezing cabbage to work much better and easier.

** She prefers to slow cook her piggies in an electric roaster.

ABOUT DEBRA

DEBRA ULLRICK is a New York Times best-selling author, who lived and worked on cattle ranches with her hubby of forty years and their only daughter. Besides writing and reading, she loves classic cars, hot rods, racing, monster trucks and feeding wild birds. Debra loves hearing from her readers. You can follow, find, or contact Debra on Twitter, Facebook, her website www.debraullrick.com or email her at christianromancewriter@gmail.com.

AN AMISH GIFT

BY MARTA PERRY

Annie Fisher thumped the rolling pin down on the noodle dough for the chicken potpie and immediately regretted it. She shouldn't let her frustration turn into tough noodles in her family's favorite meal.

She glanced at the clock. Eli hadn't come into the farmhouse at all today, moving between the furniture shop he loved and the chores on the dairy farm his father had turned over to him.

It was too much to expect. The rebellious words repeated themselves in her mind for perhaps the hundredth time. Daad Gideon, Eli's father, had meant well – she was certain of it. He'd been a natural-born dairy farmer, and he'd always seen Eli's shop as nothing more than a sideline. And things weren't so bad when he and Eli's mother were in the *grossdaadi* house that they'd added onto the farmhouse years ago.

But this spring Eli's parents had left on an extended visit to Eli's sister in Ohio, and without his father's help, Eli was running himself ragged trying to do everything. Annie had begun to feel as if they were strangers, seeing each other only at mealtime, when the children claimed their *daadi's* attention.

What had happened to the cheerful chatter and the shared laughter in their marriage? Was it ever coming back, or were they going to drift further and further apart until there was nothing between them but emptiness?

If only Eli would let her help him. Annie blinked back the tears she didn't want to let drop on the dough. Each time she'd offered to share the work, Eli had insisted she had enough to do, taking care of their four *kinder*, the garden, and the house. It was his job to deal with the farm and the business, he'd insist. He didn't need her help. And each time he'd said it, she felt more shut out.

The back screen door slammed as Abigail and Sarah ran in from school, chattering away a mile a minute about their day. At six and seven, they were as alike as if they were twins, with Abigail beginning a sentence and Sarah finishing it, as often as not.

"Peter Stolzfus pushed Sarah to get a cookie first—" Abigail exclaimed.

"And Teacher Sally said he had to sit in the corner," Sarah completed, her blue eyes as round as saucers at the thought.

"I know you would never push anyone." Annie touched her small daughter's cheek. "That would be unkind, ain't so?"

Sarah nodded solemnly. "It made me sad. But I forgave him, and he turned the jump rope for me at recess."

"*Gut.* I'm glad." Glad, too, that her children's problems were so easily solved.

The thud of small feet announced that four-year-old Joshua was up from his nap, and a wail from the baby's room proclaimed that little William was awake as well. Annie hurried up the stairs to fetch Will, grabbing Joshua on the way to insist that he put his shoes on. In a moment, she was caught up in dealing with the children and getting supper on the table, forced to shove her worries about Eli to the back of her mind in the usual daily rush.

The girls had rung the dinner bell twice, and Annie had

started ladling the potpie into an earthenware bowl, before she heard the creak of the porch step that announced Eli's arrival. She glanced toward the door, her heart giving a little lurch as he appeared, his wheat-colored hair and beard ruffled by the wind, his broad shoulders seeming to sag a bit with weariness.

Annie forced a smile to her lips, knowing Eli wouldn't like it if she mentioned something about how tired he looked. The *kinder* rushed toward him, all trying to talk at once, while little William banged on the highchair tray as if to attract his *daadi's* attention. Often at a moment like this, their gazes would meet over the little ones' heads, and they would share an unspoken communication. A moment of connection. But not today.

It's because he's so tired, she assured herself, wanting to believe it.

Eli seemed to listen to the children's chatter with only half an ear while he washed up. When Sarah tugged at his sleeve, trying to tell her story, he frowned. "*Ja*, enough."

She took a step back, her eyes filling with tears. Before Annie could intervene, though, Eli reached out to draw his daughter close for a quick hug. "*Ach*, I didn't mean to scold. Let me get clean, and then we'll talk over supper. Your *mammi* made something *gut*, I think."

"Chicken potpie," Abigail said, bouncing a little. "It's my favorite."

"Mine, too," Joshua said. "Not just yours."

"It's everyone's favorite," Annie said firmly. "Now sit at the table so we can eat it."

Eli turned back to the sink without a word, and she felt unaccountably bereft. Once again, the quick exchange of glances was missing – the look that seemed to bond them together in understanding without a word being spoken. *What is wrong with us?*

After the silent prayer that started the meal, the *kinder* dove into their supper as if they hadn't eaten in days. The girls, at least, seemed to have mastered the art of eating and talking at the same time, and they monopolized the conversation with their account of what had happened in school. Spooning noodles into Will's mouth, Annie listened, her heart aching.

Eli was barely attending, seeming preoccupied with some inner worry. How long would it be before the little ones began feeling as cut off from him as she did? When they were finished, the *kinder* scattered to do their chores. She put Will down on a rug in the corner of the kitchen where she could watch him while she did the dishes. Eli rose, stretched wearily and headed for the door.

"Do you have to go out again already?" The question came out without thought. She wished she could take it back, but it was too late.

Eli paused. "I guess not." He turned back, frowning a little. "I picked up the mail on my way in. There's a letter from my *mamm*."

"What does she have to say?" And when were they coming back, so Eli could get some relief from the workload he was carrying?

"It seems Daad had a bad spell with his heart."

The words, combined with the expression on Eli's face, wiped every other thought from her mind.

"How bad is it?" She went to him quickly, resting her hand on his arm. "Is he in the hospital?"

"Only overnight. It seems he was being stubborn about going to the doctor in spite of the pain, so Mamm had to give him one of her lectures." Eli's face lightened slightly. "That got him moving."

"It would." Mamm Rebecca was a soft-spoken woman, but when she got upset enough to lecture her family, they listened, well aware that her gentle façade hid a will of iron. "Will he be all right?"

"Mamm says yes, but it will take time. And he might never be able to get back to all he used to do." Eli seemed to make an effort to straighten his shoulders. "So the farm depends on me."

Annie hadn't realized until that moment how much she'd been looking forward to her in-laws' return and to having Eli's *daad* taking on some of the burden again.

"But Eli . . ."

He frowned, as if already disapproving of whatever she might say. "There's no point in arguing. It's what I have to do."

"But not on your own," she protested. "It's too much for you. You need help."

"I'm fine," he said shortly, heading toward the door. "Stop fussing, Annie. I can handle everything."

It was what she'd expected him to say. He took his responsibility to care for family matters seriously. But he probably didn't even think about the cost they would all be paying for his stubborn refusal to let anyone help him.

Later, coming downstairs after the young ones had been tucked in bed, Annie heard the back door. Eli was in the house at last. Perhaps now he could relax, and they could talk the way they used to – she in her rocking chair with her mending, he in his big chair reading the paper.

But Eli didn't seem to be leaving the kitchen, and finally, Annie went to see what he was doing. She found him sitting at the kitchen table, the gas light overhead bringing out glints of gold in his hair as he bent over the papers he had spread out in front of him.

"More paperwork?" she asked, resting her hands lightly on his shoulders. They felt as solid as a rock under the cotton of his shirt.

"*Ja.*" He rubbed his forehead. "Seems like half the time of running a dairy farm is spent on paperwork. If it's not records for the dairy that buys the milk, it's forms from the government."

"That's what your *daad* always said." She hesitated, but she had to offer, even though she knew the answer. "Why don't you let me help with those? I can fill them out."

"No." He snapped out the word, and she felt his shoulders hunch under her hands. "You have enough of your own to do."

Annie stood looking down at him, her heart twisting in her

chest in almost a physical pain. His thick hair curled a little against the strong column of his neck, stubbornly refusing to lay flat. *Stubborn* – that was the word, all right. Emotion flared in her, so sudden and unaccustomed that it took her a moment to recognize it. Anger. She was so angry she wanted to shake him.

"No!" Her voice shook. "Is that all you can say?"

Eli swung around in his chair, looking at her in blank astonishment.

"Now, you listen to me, Eli Fisher! You are being too stubborn for your own good. You're trying to do the farm work that usually takes two people to do and to run your furniture business as well. It's too much. And every time I offer you help, you say no. You're going to drive yourself into exhaustion. And don't tell me that your *daad* didn't accept help because I know perfectly well that your *mamm* worked right alongside of him until you were old enough to take over. So why won't you let me help?"

He stood so quickly that the chair rocked and nearly fell. "That's why, all right? That's why I didn't want you to help. I saw Mamm working so hard, sitting here every night doing the bookkeeping and taking care of all of us besides. I didn't want you to have to do the same thing. It's too much to expect."

He's used the same words she had when she'd thought of him running the farm by himself, and a rush of love flooded through her.

"*Ach*, Eli, you are being so foolish. Don't you know that your *mamm* was doing what she wanted to? She and your *daad* are partners. They share everything. The work and the joy. That's a gift they give each other. When you don't let me help, I feel . . . shut out." She stumbled over the words, but they must be said. "I feel you don't need me."

For a long moment, Eli just stared at her, realization dawning in his eyes. Then he reached out and touched her cheek. "Annie, I didn't mean it. I never meant that. Of course, I need you. I was just trying to . . ."

He stopped. Shook his head. And then he reached out and

gently pulled her to him. Annie leaned into his chest, loving the warmth and strength of him, her heart full.

"I'm sorry." He whispered the words against her hair. "I love you, Annie. Never doubt that. I didn't realize I was shutting you out."

She wrapped her arms around him, feeling as if she'd brought him home from someplace far away. "Just don't do that ever again."

A little bubble of laughter escaped on a wave of pure joy. "I guess I had to learn from your mother how to lecture."

She felt his lips curve into a smile against her cheek.

"The men in the family have hard heads, ain't so? We need a lecture now and then."

Eli drew away from her, just enough so that he could look into her face. "You're right. Whatever we have to do, we'll figure it out together. We are partners, now and always."

A NOTE FROM MARTA

Chicken Potpie and similar noodle-based recipes are dear to me because they remind me of my heritage. The Pennsylvania Dutch – who are actually of German-speaking descent, not Dutch! – have long been noted for cooking wonderful dishes made from the simplest ingredients. They use the harvest of their farms and orchards. One of my earliest memories is of my mother rising early on Sunday mornings so she could roll out the homemade noodles before we left for church. Making and sharing these familiar foods is like going home again.

CHICKEN POTPIE

2 cups cooked chicken, diced
1 quart chicken stock
2 tablespoon parsley
Dough:
1 cup flour
1 egg
¼ teaspoon baking powder
Small amount of milk

Prepare the dough by mixing together flour, egg and baking powder. Add a small amount of milk as needed to make a soft dough. Roll the dough out thinly on a floured board. Allow to rest for 30 minutes. Cut the dough into 1 ½-inch squares.

Combine chicken, chicken stock and parsley in a kettle. Bring to a boil. Drop the potpie squares gently into the boiling broth, stirring. Reduce heat and allow to simmer 20 to 30 minutes, adding additional broth if needed to keep from sticking. Makes four servings.

ABOUT MARTA

With over six million copies of her books in print, **MARTA PERRY** credits her Pennsylvania Dutch ancestry and a lifetime in the Pennsylvania countryside for the Amish stories she writes. She and her husband live in a centuries-old farmhouse in a central Pennsylvania valley. Connect with Marta through her web site, www.martaperry.com, or Facebook. Email her at marta@martaperry.com for a signed bookmark and a brochure of Pennsylvania Dutch recipes.

THE GUYS-ONLY GOURMET BIRTHDAY DINNER

BY ARLENE JAMES

"He's a *cook*," Austin said, imbuing the last word with all the disgust that a seven-year-old could muster. Correction, an eight-year-old. It was Austin's eighth birthday, not a very happy one for a boy with a new house, new neighborhood, new school and – worst of all – a new dad.

"He's a chef," Veronica told him, sitting on the edge of her son's bed. "Gordon may have been a cook in the Army, but now he's a chef. There's a difference."

Salary-wise, the difference was huge, but to this one little boy, money and security, even his mom's happiness, meant nothing. Gordon Halbert understood that he could never measure up to the boy's late father, Capt. Jason Horn. To Austin, the Army didn't equate to the Marine Corps, enlisted men didn't deserve the same respect as officers, and siblings, especially two younger *stepsisters*, rated somewhere below pets.

In the six months that Gordon and Veronica had been married, Austin had learned to control his rudeness, but his disdain had remained. Now Veronica feared the boy's reaction when he learned that she was, unexpectedly, pregnant. Personally, Gordon couldn't have been happier about the marriage or the baby. After his daughters' mother had walked out on them and then had died while driving drunk, he'd never expected to find a woman like Veronica.

They'd met in church, and her experience as a military wife had given them a common frame of reference. She'd been grieving the death of her husband in Afghanistan, and he'd been wrangling two little girls. He'd known right away that he wanted to be with her, and he told her that he'd prayed her into love with him. Now if only prayer could yield the same result with her, *their*, son. He didn't want to replace the boy's father, only to make his own place in Austin's life and heart. Fortunately, he did have some tools with which to work.

"Aw, come on, Austin," Gordon said, ambling into the room. "It'll be fun. An all-guy, gourmet birthday dinner. Just you, me, Uncle Bonner and Spud."

"He's not my uncle, and what kind of name is *Spud*?"

"Spud's a nickname. Your grand—uh, my parents own a restaurant, and their world revolves around food, so sometimes they give *foodie* nicknames."

Victoria stood and smiled. "The girls and I are going now. We'll be home in time for cake and ice cream." Ignoring her son's folded arms, she bent to kiss him. "Have fun!"

She sailed into Gordon's arms, pressed her luscious self against him, her arms about his neck, and kissed him fully on the mouth before whispering into his ear, "Praying for you."

"Thanks, babe," he called as she escaped. He clapped his hands together. "Okay. Let's get with it. We've got to chop that tree."

For the first time since the conversation had begun, Austin looked at him. "Huh?"

"Chopped Tree Casserole. It's a Halbert family rite of passage, and a military favorite. I've cooked it for generals. So get the ax, dude, and let's chop the tree."

As hoped, Austin stood and headed for the garage. What

boy could resist the lure of a sharp blade? Gordon had counted on that fact of nature and had made sure to leave the small ax within reach.

"I'm sure the captain taught you how to properly handle that," he said as Austin reached for the slick red handle. "Always carrying it near the head and not swinging by the handle, with the blade pointed away from your body and anyone with you."

Austin readjusted his grip without a word. Gordon led him to the far corner of the property, where a spindly honey mesquite and was dying because it required less water than the landscaping plants surrounding it. Gordon left several bowls in a cardboard box nearby.

"Now, let's see." He rubbed his chin. "Your mom doesn't want us digging up the yard looking for worms, so we'll substitute macaroni. It's pretty standard. Had to buy the mushrooms. Just can't find them many places in Texas. So we need the dirt, leaves, bark and wood chips."

Austin stared at him for a full five seconds. "Dirt?"

"Well, sand is better, but..." Gordon gestured helplessly. "Around here, we have to settle for dirt. Don't worry, though. I spice it up real nice and cover the whole thing with cheese."

Austin rolled his eyes, not buying it. Yet.

"So, what do you want to do?" Gordon asked. "Chop the tree or sift the dirt?"

"I'll chop."

Reminding himself that the emergency room stood only blocks away, Gordon tried to appear unconcerned. "Okay. Keep your vee tight, your angle straight and your swing smooth. But you already know that."

He moved off, crouched and filled one of the bowls with sifted dirt. Meanwhile, the ax *thunked* and *thunked* against the spindly mesquite trunk. Finally, Gordon took pity on the boy and straightened.

"That should do it. How are you coming?"

Austin let the ax head drop to the ground and leaned against the handle, breathing hard. In late September, Texas weather remained warm enough to raise a sweat, even with easy labor.

"Need a drink?" Gordon tossed a water bottle toward Austin.

The boy let the ax handle fall and caught the bottle. Wrenching off the top, he slugged back a long draught. Gordon took over for him with the ax, cutting a chink in the slender bole. After deepening the cut, he wedged the blade into it, anchored it with his foot, grasped the narrow trunk above the cut and pulled it toward him. The trunk broke with a snap. The thing was little more than a dried twig, but he wasn't above showing off, and the look in Austin's eyes encouraged him.

Using his knife, he stripped the bark and then used the ax to chop chunks of the fragrant inner wood, while Austin plucked leaves from the branches. They filled their remaining bowls, stacked them in the box and carried the box and their tools back to the house. The remains of the tree could be disposed of later.

After washing up in the kitchen, they shared a cool drink before getting down to business. Gordon loved his kitchen, from its hulking gas range to the pots hanging over the work island. For him, the kitchen was the heart of the home, and he would bond with his stepson here or not at all. Humming, he put on a pot of water to boil, unpacked the bowls and buttered a large casserole dish. Austin watched suspiciously as he took cheese, mushrooms and sour cream from the refrigerator and then collected chicken broth, macaroni, olive oil and spices from the pantry. When he pulled out his knives, the boy erupted.

"We can't eat that!"

"But Chopped Tree Casserole is a Halbert family tradition. A rite of passage. No Halbert male grows into adulthood without eating it. Army generals eat it. True, we have to make substitutions from time to time, but..."

"Substitutions? Like what?"

"Well . . ." Gordon pretended to consider. "The dirt around

101

here really isn't optimal. I've used breadcrumbs successfully."

The boy's relief was palpable. "Breadcrumbs." He found some in the pantry.

Gordon filled a colander with leaves and carried it to the sink.

"Have you ever eaten a mesquite leaf?" the boy asked.

"No. Don't think so. We usually prefer pin oak."

"Well, how do you know it'll work? It might be poison!"

"People cook with mesquite all the time," Gordon said, "but you didn't care for the mesquite smoked shrimp we had the other night, did you?"

The boy shook his head.

"Hmm. Guess we could use broccoli. Who would know, right?"

Austin didn't particularly care for broccoli, but he accepted that compromise. "The wood. That's mesquite, too."

"Once it's soaked in broth, it tastes just like chicken."

"Then just use chicken."

"We do have some cooked chicken," Gordon mused.

Next, they had substituted bacon for bark, and then it was time for the knives to come out. Austin allowed Gordon to show him how to chop the mushrooms and broccoli.

When Bonner and Spud arrived, there was a moment of awkwardness. Gordon's older brother had come with ingredients for a salad and a loaf of freshly baked Italian bread. As no breath of subtlety had ever touched Bonner, he glanced at Austin and said, "So, this is the hero's bratty son, huh?"

"Captain Horn was, indeed, a hero," Gordon replied calmly.

Spud, bless him, papered over the indelicate remark by introducing himself as, "Bonner's bratty boy." An unusually wise ten-year-old, he put out his pudgy hand and said, "Happy birthday. My name's really Bruce, but everyone calls me Spud 'cause I'm built like a potato. I take after my mom that way. Makes me a killer linebacker."

Bonner cuffed him harmlessly. "Hey! Your mother is the loveliest 300-pound woman walking this earth." He shrugged at Austin. "So I prefer prime rib to chicken wings."

Austin turned to Gordon. "What does that make mom?"

"Filet mignon."

Austin raised an approving brow. What likely impressed him more was that Spud had come with his own set of kitchen knives. When the boy unrolled the leather case and chose a serrated blade to slice tomatoes, Austin goggled.

"Got 'em for my ninth," Spud told him, moving on to radishes.

"First comes Chopped Tree Casserole," said Bonner, "then a year of instruction, and if you're up to it, Papa Halbert will give you your own set of knives."

"He started with the chopping already," Gordon pointed out.

"Yeah?" Bonner said. "That's good. Nice, equal sizing."

Austin beamed. Gordon caught Bonner's eye, telegraphing his gratitude. The four of them worked quickly, putting the meal together. Soon the boys were giggling and flinging bits of carrot at each other. Gordon made a centerpiece out of the unused chopped-tree elements and had the boys set the table. By the time the casserole was ready, the two were fast friends.

Gordon waited to see if Austin would admit he liked the gussied up macaroni and cheese or would revert to his ambivalent self. It's difficult to dislike something tasty that you've helped cook, though.

"Thish ish delishush," he proclaimed around a full mouth.

Bonner had declared that Guys-Only rules applied, and normal table manners could be temporarily suspended.

"Pity the women folk can't eat this," Bonner opined.

Spud whispered to Austin, "We let Mom when no one else is around."

Austin nodded, and Bonner flicked Spud's ear as the brothers traded amused looks.

Veronica and the girls came in then, their arms filled with birthday gifts.

"Ice cweam!" Tilly cried, clapping her hands.

"Chopped Tree," Sarah surmised, bellying up to the table.

Veronica came up to kiss Gordon. "It smells wonderful."

"Not for you girls," he warned with a wink.

"How did it go?" she mouthed.

He gave her a surreptitious thumbs-up and got a bright smile before she placed her bounty in front of Austin. They enjoyed their cake and ice cream, and then Austin opened his gifts, which included the martial arts clothing and lessons he'd so craved. The boy seemed happier than he had in six months.

Later that night as they tucked him into bed, Gordon didn't hang back as far as usual, but he didn't sit on the bed with Veronica yet, either. Only time would tell how much headway they'd made today. As they were about to leave the room, Austin voiced the concern that Gordon had sensed building in him.

"Thank you for the Chopped Tree Casserole, but . . . I'm not a Halbert."

"Well, not *legally*," Gordon admitted, his heart pounding, "but that doesn't matter."

"All the rest of this family are Halberts," he snapped. "*I'm* a Horn."

Gordon thought it over. "You could hyphenate. Be a Halbert-Horn. That way, you don't lose your first dad's name, and you have your second dad's name, too."

The smile on that kid's face would warm Gordon's heart for years to come.

"Yeah. Austin Halbert-Horn. That'll work."

Being a *second dad* was a good thing, after all, a very good thing.

A NOTE FROM ARLENE

I created this recipe to get my kids to eat broccoli and mushrooms, which I had to chop finely at first. They believed they were eating chopped trees in their mac n' cheese. Once you've eaten chopped trees, you can eat anything, right? This casserole became one of our favorites and my stand-by for potlucks and sick folks. Today, one of my sons uses store-bought mac n' cheese and makes his on the stovetop, substituting milk for sour cream and butter for olive oil, while another covers the entire casserole with bacon strips. To each his own, I say, so long as you get those "trees" in there.

ARLENE'S CHOPPED TREE CASSEROLE

12 ounces macaroni
½ cup olive oil
4 cups cubed, cooked chicken
10 slices bacon, cooked & crumbled (divided use; don't overcook)
2 cups chicken broth
1 ½ cups sour cream
3 medium heads fresh broccoli
1 cup breadcrumbs
½ teaspoon garlic powder
½ teaspoon salt
1 teaspoon paprika
½ teaspoon ground pepper
1 ½ cups mushrooms, chopped
4 cups shredded Monterey Jack Cheese

Butter a large casserole dish or spray with cooking spray. Set aside. Preheat oven to 400 degrees F. While oven is heating, boil water in large pot for macaroni. Follow package directions. While water is heating, rinse broccoli and cut stalks from core. Cook them in large saucepan over medium-high heat until tender, about 8 minutes from the time the water starts to boil. Drain broccoli and return to saucepan. Using two sharp knives or kitchen shears, cut into small pieces. When macaroni is done just to al dente stage, drain and return to large pot. Pour olive oil over it and stir to coat.

Add broccoli, cubed chicken, chopped mushrooms, and 3 tablespoons of the crumbled bacon; stir. In large saucepan, heat chicken broth to boiling. Add salt, pepper and garlic powder. Remove from heat. Whisk sour cream in chicken broth mixture, followed by cheese. Stir until cheese is melted. Dump macaroni/chicken/broccoli mixture into casserole dish and level with back of large spoon or spatula. Pour chicken broth/sour cream/cheese mixture evenly over top, stirring and leveling. Combine breadcrumbs and paprika. Sprinkle breadcrumbs evenly over top of casserole. Arrange crumbled bacon evenly around dish edges. Bake 10-20 minutes or until dish is heated through. Top appears a bit browned and "crusted," and bacon is crisp. Yield: 10 servings.

ABOUT ARLENE

ARLENE JAMES is the author of more than 85 novels. Publishing steadily for nearly four decades, she has concentrated on Inspirational Romance for several years. She and her husband, artist James E. Rather, have traveled much of the world and, after living in the Dallas/Fort Worth, Texas, area for 33 years, now call northwest Arkansas home. She can be contacted via email at deararlenejames@gmail.com or on Facebook.

IN THE MARKET FOR LOVE

BY GAIL GAYMER MARTIN

Carly Darnell grimaced at the run in her only pair of taupe pantyhose. Why did it always happen on a busy day? She shrugged, adding it to her list of annoyances.

Trying to think positively, she found a purpose for her problem. If she had to stop at the store for stockings, she might as well pick up a few groceries. Seizing a scratch pad, she jotted a list of things she needed. But when she lowered the pencil, her mind gave a kick.

"Corn tortillas." She looked heavenward, pleased that she'd remembered. For dinner, she wanted to make Enchilada Pie, one of her favorite dishes, and she'd almost forgotten one of the main ingredients. After scribbling that last item on the list, she reached for her handbag. Though the stop would delay her, with good timing and a small blessing, she could still make it to her morning meeting.

Before she could take a step, her telephone rang. She grabbed the receiver and gave a rattled "hello."

"Carly? It's Marianne. Could I ask a big favor?"

"What do you need? I'm on my way out the door. I have a nine-thirty meeting, and I have to stop at the supermarket first."

"Supermarket? Great!"

From Marianne's excitement, Carly was almost convinced that she'd said the secret word to win some grand prize.

"Could you get a couple cans of Doggie Chow for Rex? I don't have the car today, and he won't eat just anything. I'd really appreciate it."

Carly rolled her eyes. No secret word. No grand prize. And on top of everything, she had to cater to a neighbor's dog with finicky tastes. But remembering the Golden Rule, she relented. "Sure, Marianne. I'll drop it by after work."

After ending the call, she locked the house and headed for the market. She wheeled into the parking lot, skidding against the curb. To avoid losing a prime parking spot, she pressed the gas pedal, managing to avoid a shocked-looking shopper, who dodged out of her way.

Slightly rattled, Carly hurried inside the store, snatched a cart and tackled the first aisle. Canned tuna. Soup. She tossed the cans into her basket and struggled to round the corner, fighting the cart, which had a mind of its own.

In the next aisle, she spied the pantyhose display. Her gaze shifted down the rows of packaged hosiery. Nude. Beige. Black. No taupe. As she crouched to check the bottom rack, a whack and thud rocked her from behind and knocked her to her knees. "Hey!"

"Whoa. Sorry."

The amused, deep voice behind her ruffled the hairs on her neck, despite the fresh ache to her backside. She turned her head toward the speaker and spotted a shopping cart connected to an embarrassed-looking man . . . make that a good-looking, embarrassed man, wearing jeans and a two-tone, three-button shirt. He stared down at her with a pair of glinting ocean-blue eyes.

His full lips lifted then, flashing even, white teeth. "I bet that hurt."

As she shot upward, Carly rammed her elbow into his basket. She frowned, massaging her funny bone while wondering where it got that ridiculous name.

"Apparently, this isn't my day." She tried to hide her mortification and hoped to regain her poise despite his warm gaze addling her. She motioned toward the hosiery rack. "No taupe, and I have an important meeting. I need to look good." As she blurted out her stocking woes, heat rose up her neck.

The stranger shifted his focus to the display and raked his fingers through his thick, fawn-colored hair. In a moment, he reached for the top rack, pulled out a package and scanned the wrapper. "Here they are. Taupe." He looked from the plastic covering to her frame, sizing her from head to toe. "It says five-feet-three to five-five and ninety-six to one hundred fifteen pounds. Size A. These should fit."

With a wink, he handed her the package. Her flush sizzled. Following a mumbled thank you, she made her escape and maneuvered the cart down the aisle while glancing at him over her shoulder. When she caught him grinning at her, she grumbled under her breath. Why did she always run into attractive hunks at the grocery store or in an office building elevator? Why couldn't it happen at a party where, with time and cleverness, she might capture an introduction?

As she searched the aisles for her final items, she couldn't keep from studying passing shoppers, hoping to spot the nameless man with those amazing eyes again. Her tight schedule prodded her to stop lollygagging. She was in the market for groceries, not for romance.

At the checkout, she remembered the dog food and retraced her steps, trying to recall Rex-the-picky-eater's brand. When she reached the pet-food aisle, she scanned the labels: Puppy Dinner, Butcher Bites, Doggie Bits. Doggie . . . It had something to do with Doggie. Doggie Chews? No. Sensing she was being watched, she turned and spotted her pantyhose hero trailing behind her and eyeing the same cans.

When he lifted his head, he saw her and winked. "Need any help? I seem to have an uncanny knack." He emphasized the *can* in "uncanny," grabbing two of the containers from the shelf and shifting them from hand to hand.

She chuckled. "You do have a way with words, Mr. . . ."

"Rawlings." He set the cans on the shelf. "Brad Rawlings." His smile echoed in his voice.

"Carly Brackston, I think." She grinned. "I can't remember much today. I was on my way to check out when I remembered dog food, and now I'm blank on the brand."

"Let's see." He dragged his index finger along the row and then paused. "King likes Doggie Chow." He grabbed a can from the display.

"That's it. Doggie Chow. Rex won't eat anything else."

"What a coincidence. Our dogs have the same discriminating taste."

"Seems that way. Thanks again." She dropped the cans into her basket without correcting his assumption. What harm was there in allowing him to think she had a dog? As she backed away, her belligerent cart planted its wheels into the floor tile, refusing to budge.

Brad flashed a beguiling grin and knelt beside her cart. He rotated the wheels, and they turned, finally cooperating.

"Thanks. Again." She gazed into his striking face. "I'm in a terrible hurry, but it was nice to meet you."

She paid for her purchases and hurried to the parking lot. When she reached the car, she tossed her handbag on the bumper and dug the key from her pocket while balancing the two bags against her chest. With the packages safely inside the trunk, she closed the lid with a sigh. Her watch read nine-ten. She had twenty minutes to drive to work and change her pantyhose if she hoped to make the meeting on time. To Carly's surprise, traffic cooperated, and she arrived with two minutes to spare.

She didn't miss her handbag until she gathered her belongings at the end of the day. Her panic rose as she searched her desk and the conference room with zero results. Then she remembered. The market. Her bumper. She hurried from her office to the parking lot and raced to the grocery store.

Her heart sank as she scanned the parking area with no luck. Foolish. No one would pass an abandoned handbag and leave it. They'd take it or— With a fragment of hope, she darted inside to the manager's station, but she didn't receive the answer she'd hoped for. She left the market empty-handed.

Her mind still whirling, Carly drove home, angry at her carelessness. She prepared herself for a long evening of telephone calls to credit card companies. Finally home, she gathered the groceries and piled them into the cabinet. Only the dog food remained on the counter. She would worry about Rex's food after her calls. She located a pencil, tore off a piece of note paper and plopped into a kitchen chair to write the list of calls she needed to make.

Before she finished, the doorbell interrupted her thoughts. She raised her shoulders and released a sigh. Of course, Marianne would want the dog food. Carly pulled herself up from the chair. She wasn't in the mood to share her missing-handbag story, so she hoped to make her neighbor's visit a brief one. She grabbed the cans and hurried to the front door.

Ocean-colored eyes gazed at her through the screen. Brad Rawlings. Right at her front door. He clutched her purse in one hand and a can of Doggie Chow in the other.

She gaped at him as questions filled her mind.

"The handbag doesn't match my shoes," he explained, "so I thought I'd return it." He held the purse out to her.

When her senses returned, she opened the screen. "Oh, you found it. What a relief! I could kiss you." Her eyes widened as her comment echoed in her head. "I . . ."

"If that's how you express your gratitude, I brought dog food, too." He slipped the purse into her already full arms, but he continued holding the dog food.

She stared at the can, her thoughts moving from his eyes to her purse to the Doggie Chow, before she pushed the door open wider. "Would you like to come in?"

"I'd better. I don't want the neighbors to talk when I collect that kiss you promised me." He gave her a sheepish look.

"Have I gotten carried away?"

"Yes, a bit." But her pulse skipped as she imagined herself in his arms. "How did you find my bag?" She beckoned him to follow and led him to the kitchen.

"I spotted your purse on the ground after you pulled away. I thought about turning it in, but it seemed safer with me." He paused and lifted an eyebrow. "Anyway, how else would I see you again?"

The familiar hot flush crept along her hairline. "You've rescued me a number of times today." She dropped her handbag on the counter, still juggling the dog food cans she'd carried to the door. "I really appreciate your returning my purse. But I don't understand the dog food."

Brad chuckled. "I was fairly confident you wouldn't bite me when I showed up at your door, but I wasn't sure about Rex. It's a peace offering." He glanced around as if waiting for the dog to bound into the room. Finally, he cleared his throat and shifted from one foot to the other. "I want to be honest. I don't really own a dog. I grabbed the can, hoping you wouldn't think I was following you."

"But you were?"

"Guilty as charged."

Amused, she set her cans on the counter and accepted the one he offered. "Since you're coming clean, I have to admit that I don't have a dog either, but it's a long and boring story."

Frowning, he eyed all the cans.

"There is a Rex, though. And I know he'll appreciate your gift. He's finicky."

"Aha, that explains it." He shrugged, hinting that he really didn't understand at all. "Can I look forward to a full explanation . . . let's say over dinner?"

Reining in her galloping heart, she averted her gaze.

"What do you say?" he pressed.

When she faced him, her pulse reared like a mare out of control. "Well, I—"

"You haven't eaten, have you?"

"No, I haven't."

Unbelievable. Who'd have thought she'd meet her possible dream man in the pantyhose aisle? She drew in a calming breath. "I'd planned to make Enchilada Pie, but I suppose that could wait."

She swallowed her excitement. "I'd love to have dinner. And just for the record, I'm not finicky at all."

"That's good news." He sent her a playful grin. "And to resolve the Enchilada Pie issue, I'd be happy to join you another day when you're making it . . . if that's not being too presumptuous."

"Presumptuous. No. But taking a chance? Yes. You might hate me after tonight."

He tilted his head, his eyes flashing with amusement. "I doubt that. Any girl who volunteers to buy a finicky dog's canned food and one who must wear taupe pantyhose instead of an ordinary color is my kind of woman. Thoughtful and discriminating." He winked.

"I enjoy men who are willing to help with problems. You're on for my delicious Enchilada Pie. How about tomorrow? Are you free?"

"Very."

Her heart sang. "Dinner will be at seven, but you're welcome to come earlier. You can set the table."

"It's a deal." He gestured toward the door. "Dinner? Ready?"

She grasped her purse and cradled the dog food against her chest. "I need a minute though." She steered him toward the front door. "I'd like you to meet Rex. The poor dog hasn't had his dinner yet either." She glanced at Brad over her shoulder.

With a puzzled look in his teasing eyes, he followed her.

As Carly jogged across her neighbor's lawn while Brad waited for her in the driveway, she reviewed her day, realizing that she owed Rex more than a few cans of food. Without him and his Doggie Chow, she might never have met the man with the beguiling eyes. The man of her dreams.

115

A NOTE FROM GAIL

This is a dish I love. We enjoy all kinds of Mexican food, and this one is so easy to make. It's almost like a Mexican lasagna, but easier and delicious.

ENCHILADA PIE

3 pounds lean ground chuck
Salt to taste
Pepper to taste
Garlic to taste
6 yellow corn tortillas, burrito size
1 large, finely chopped onion
2 cans of mild enchilada sauce
1 can of Mexicali corn or yellow corn
1 16-ounce package shredded cheddar cheese

Sauté meat in skillet. Season with salt, pepper and garlic. Drain fat. Place three corn tortillas in 9 by 13 pan. Layer half the meat mixture. Sprinkle on half of diced onion. Pour a half can of corn and one can of enchilada sauce over meat and half of shredded cheddar.

Top with final three tortillas, layering the other ingredients in lasagna fashion. (Tortillas, meat, onions, corn, sauce, cheese). Bake at 350 for 45 minutes. After cooked, if desired, garnish with lettuce and tomato. Option: Substitute ground beef with chicken or ground turkey for a healthier meal, and you can also use flour tortillas rather than corn.

ABOUT GAIL

Award-winning novelist, **GAIL GAYMER MARTIN** is the author of 55 contemporary Christian novels, with four million books in print. CBS local news listed Gail among the four best writers in the Detroit area. A cofounder of American Christian Fiction Writers, Gail is a speaker at churches and women's conferences. She lives in Michigan with her husband. Gail can be contacted through Facebook, Twitter or Goodreads or on her web site, www.gailgaymermartin.com.

ROSE'S OUTLAW

BY SHERRI SHACKELFORD

Troublesome Creek, Kansas, 1881

If Rose Garrison had known how the day would end, she'd have worn a different dress. Except nothing ever happened in Troublesome Creek.

Nothing. Ever.

Especially not at The End of the Line Café.

She rested her elbows on the whitewashed windowsill and stared out the freshly scrubbed panes. Six years ago, a heavy spring rain had washed out the railroad bridge. The water had taken months to recede. Impatient with the delay, the Burlington Railroad had rerouted. Without a thriving depot, the town had quickly withered.

First the blacksmith had closed, then the haberdashery. The other shops had fallen like dominoes. Only a handful of old-timers remained to patronize the few enduring businesses.

The railroad wasn't coming back.

Neither was anyone else.

A scruffy-looking man pushed through the door. Wrinkling

her nose, Rose hoped he didn't smell too bad. Her only patrons these days were gamblers from the saloon. Sometimes those fellows forgot to bathe. The newcomer shuffled across the room and slumped onto one of the benches along the wall.

Plastering a bright smile on her face, she approached his table. "Can I you get you something to eat, sir? We have beef and noodles today."

She took a discreet whiff and caught the faint aroma of sandalwood. Thank goodness for small favors.

"Angel food cake for dessert?" His voice was rusty as though he rarely spoke.

"Of course. How did you know?"

The pairing was her family's tradition. The yolks from fresh eggs were used to make the noodles, and the egg whites were reserved for baking angel food cake later in the day.

The dark-haired stranger caught her gaze. "Lucky guess."

A comforting sense of familiarity tugged at the edges of her memory. She paused, captivated by his eyes. They were fathomless and brown, almost black, and yet she sensed the barest hint of warmth. Upon closer inspection, he was much younger than she'd first assumed. His forehead was smooth, and the skin above his dark beard was weathered by the sun yet unlined by time.

She tucked a stray tendril of red hair behind her ear and smoothed a hand down her apron. "Will you be staying in town long?"

"Nope."

"What's your name?"

"Briggs."

Her stomach dipped.

Briggs. Squinting, she mentally peeled off the years and stripped away the layers of facial hair. Those eyes. How had she not recognized those eyes straight off?

Blood roared in her ears, and she stumbled back. "But . . . it can't be."

He caught her hand. "You remember me, don't you, Rose?"

She remembered him, all right. He'd been her first love, her first kiss and her first heartbreak. He'd promised to come back for her. Liar. Some things a girl couldn't forget, even if she tried. Even if she tried really, really hard.

Briggs clasped his hands on the table. "Do you still have those love letters I wrote you when we were kids?"

"Sort of," she mumbled. "I stuffed them in a box and buried the whole thing behind the outhouse, then planted stinkweed on top of the spot."

A grin lifted one corner of his mouth. "I guess I deserved that."

Physically, he was nothing like the boy she remembered. His shoulder muscles strained against his grubby shirt, and the expanse of his chest drew her admiring gaze. Judging from his clothing, the years had not treated him well. She sneaked a look at his corded forearms, and her stomach fluttered. He might have fallen on hard times, but manual labor had shaped him into a man.

She sank onto the seat opposite him. "What happened to you?"

He tugged on his scruffy beard. "I guess I've changed a bit."

"A bit." With her heart hammering in her chest, she searched his face. "Did you . . . did you find what you were searching for?"

When work had dried up in town, he'd left with a swagger in his step, determined to make it big. He'd promised to come back for her once he'd made his fortune.

"Ah, Rose." He took her hand, rubbing her palm, the rough callous of his thumb sending gooseflesh dancing up her arm. "Don't get that disappointed look in your eyes like the old days."

She snatched away her hand. "I was never disappointed."

"Sure you were. You used to look at me with those sad green eyes, like you saw the path I was heading down and you were already mourning my future."

She mentally grasped for the seedling of anger she'd

121

nurtured all of these years. "You ran with some rough boys. I was worried. We all were. Why come back now?"

"For you. I'm keeping my promise. I'm only sorry I took so long."

She stared at him in stunned silence. If his appearance was any indication, he'd lowered his standards on what it meant to make his fortune. Not that money had ever mattered to her. She would have left with him when he was just a poor boy from town.

The rear door slammed, a welcome distraction.

She scrambled from her seat, away from his undeniable draw. Despite his obvious hard luck, or maybe because of it, she sensed he'd break her heart again if she wasn't careful. And she wasn't ready to forgive him. Not now. Maybe not ever.

"I have to see to that," she said.

His gaze narrowed. "You expecting someone?"

"It's probably Pete, from the mercantile. He's delivering peaches."

She whirled and pushed through the swinging doors, nearly colliding with the twin barrels of a shotgun.

Her heart lodged in her throat.

The man holding the gun in her face was squat and soft around the middle. A patchwork beard covered his round face, and his stained hat sat at a crooked angle.

The intruder lifted his gaze above the stock, one eye squinted in concentration. "What's your name, girlie?"

"R . . . Rose."

For an agonizing moment she remained frozen like a dimwit. The swinging door whooshed behind her. She took an involuntary step back and collided with a solid wall of male chest. Fear robbed her of breath, and she sucked air into her tight lungs.

"Easy there, my Irish Rose." Briggs soothed.

The barrel lowered.

Briggs growled. "Thought we were meeting in Cimarron Springs, Smitty."

They knew each other? Her brief spark of hope

disintegrated. Briggs' rough appearance instantly made sense. He'd found success in something, all right. She recognized an outlaw when she saw one.

"Change of plans," the intruder replied.

Briggs' heavy hand landed on her shoulder, and the aroma of sandalwood soap enveloped her. The enticing scent would be forever associated with the stolen kisses they'd shared. Never again. Anger burned hot in her chest. He was a fugitive. The man she'd pined after for three years had turned outlaw.

A shout sounded from the dining room. "Anybody back there? I'm here for supper."

"Tell him you'll be right out," Briggs spoke, his rasping voice vibrating against her ear.

"I . . . I'll." She cleared her throat. "Be right out."

She swayed on her feet. A strong arm looped around her waist. The heat from Briggs' body radiated against her back.

"Relax, Rose," he whispered. "Everything will be fine."

A shiver of awareness skimmed down her spine. He'd never hurt her, that much she knew for certain. Just like she knew he'd never let the man holding the shotgun hurt her. Which meant he was here for something else. He'd finally come for her, just like he'd promised.

"Why?" she asked, imbuing a wealth of meaning and hurt into the single word. "Did you actually think I'd run off with you? Become an outlaw, too?"

"I'll explain everything later."

Smitty swiped at his nose with one hand and reached for the back of a chair.

Rose yelped and shoved past Briggs. "Do not touch my noodles!"

They were draped over every surface in the kitchen to dry. The chairs, the table, even the sink. She'd spent all morning rolling and cutting those noodles, and no one was going to ruin her hard work. Even if he did have a gun.

The outlaw straightened and brought his hands to his sides.

Briggs chuckled at her uncharacteristic show of temper. "Rose, why don't you take the fellow in the dining room a slice of pie?"

"Pie?"

His breath puffed against her temple. "Pie."

Rose nodded. At least the request gave her a purpose beyond being terrified. She made a shaky exit through the swinging door. As she bent over her task, Briggs and Smitty emerged from the kitchen.

His shotgun now at his side, Smitty cackled. "You weren't kidding, Briggs. There can't be more than twenty old-timers in this whole town. Ain't no sheriff or able-bodied men around for miles."

Dessert plate in hand, Rose approached the new customer, a man in his fifties, dressed in black, his hat slung low over his eyes. Smitty stuck out his foot and tripped her. She pitched forward and the pie sailed through the air, splattering on the customer's chest. A dollop of cinnamon-flecked apple filling oozed from his beard and dripped onto his shiny tin star.

"It's the law," Smitty hollered, raising his gun barrel.

The deputy whipped out his pistol.

Gunshots exploded. Rose's ears rang, and the pungent scent of gunpowder burned her nose.

Without giving herself time to think, she grabbed the front of Briggs' shirt. "Run. Get out of here."

He caught her wrists against his chest. "No."

"You fool!" She spun around and splayed her arms. "Don't shoot. He's not one of them."

The deputy pushed back his hat with the smoking tip of his pistol. "I know."

Briggs was no green youth, yet he feared his beating heart would burst from his chest. Rose had defended him. She'd tried to save him. There was hope for the two of them. There had to be.

The deputy holstered his gun. "Briggs here is a Federal Marshal. He infiltrated their gang." The man stood and crossed to Smitty's prone form. "Too bad I had to kill the ol' fellow. Bet he had more secrets to tell."

124

Briggs shrugged. "He didn't give you any choice."

Looking stunned, Rose warily eyed him.

"You see, Rose," he said. "I told you everything would be fine."

"You're a Federal Marshal?"

"Yep." He studied her face. Was she angry or relieved? "Look Rose, I'm sorry. Smitty wasn't supposed to follow me here."

The deputy grunted. "Good thing I was tracking him. You nearly got this poor woman killed."

Rose grimaced at the fallen outlaw. "You were pretending the whole time?"

"We set a trap for the others in Cimarron Springs. I've been running with those boys for two years. Since they're all caught, we can be together."

The sharp smack across his cheek caught him unaware.

He rubbed out the pain. "What was that for?"

"Why you no good, lying, double-crossing." She paused for breath. "Bad kisser!"

The deputy straightened. "Looks like I interrupted something."

Rose socked his arm several times. "I waited for you. I waited and waited and waited."

"You don't have to wait any longer." He dropped to one knee and grasped her cold hands. "Marry me, Rose. Come to Washington. I've made my fortune. Maybe not a fortune, but I'm set. The president is giving me an award and a promotion."

Smitty muttered, and his eyes popped open. "I ain't dead, you idiots."

The deputy kicked away his shotgun and peeled back the outlaw's shirt. "If that don't beat all. The bullet hit his flask."

"It hurts like the dickens." Smitty groaned.

Rose glared at the outlaw. "Shhh!"

Briggs swallowed around the lump in his throat. She hadn't said "no" yet, but she was holding his hands in a painful grip that turned his fingers purple.

"I would have come with you before," she said quietly.

"When you had nothing. You never had to prove yourself to me."

"I had to, Rose, don't you see? I needed to become a man worthy of your love."

Her eyes misted. "Really?"

The wonder in her face sent his heartbeat tripping.

Smitty pushed up on one elbow. "Running with outlaws. How's that honorable?"

"Shhh!" Rose and Briggs ordered.

The outlaw huffed and collapsed on his back once more.

Rose loosened her grip on Briggs' fingers. "If I agree to marry you, do you promise you will never put yourself in danger again?"

"I promise. Mostly."

She crossed her arms over her chest and paced. He waited. She paced some more.

After an eternity, she paused before him. "Then the answer is yes. I will marry you."

He leapt to his feet, but she planted a restraining hand on his chest. "Not so fast. You owe me three years of courting."

"How about three weeks?"

"Three months."

"Ah, Rose. I've been loving you for three years. Doesn't that count?"

Her expression grew bashful. "I forgot about your supper. You must be famished. I'll heat up your beef and noodles."

He swept her close and bent her back over his arm. "Supper can wait. Don't you have something to tell me?"

She cupped his cheek. "I never stopped loving you, either."

"That's better."

As the deputy dragged Smitty outside, Briggs kissed her with all the love he'd been holding in for three years.

When he released her, she stumbled away, looking muddled. "I lied."

His heart dropped.

"You're not a bad kisser." She flashed a saucy grin. "Let's keep that courtship to three weeks."

Briggs cradled her in his arms once more. "Now that's something we can both agree on."

A NOTE FROM SHERRI

My Great-aunt Alyce was raised during the Great Depression and never wasted anything! When she made egg noodles, she always baked angel food cake with the leftover egg whites. This recipe brings back fond memories of my aunt and her delicious, thrifty ways.

ROSE'S EGG NOODLES

6 egg yolks
6 tablespoons water
3 cups flour (approximate)
½ teaspoons salt

Mix egg yolks and water. Stir together salt and flour. Heap flour on clean surface. Make well in center. Add egg yolk mixture. Combine and knead until an elastic dough forms. (Add a few extra tablespoons of water or flour as necessary.) Divide the dough into three balls. Roll each out into paper-thin rectangle. Dust with flour and roll up jellyroll style. Slice off slender strips, then unroll. Makes 1 pound.

To cook noodles: Bring 3 quarts water to a boil and cook 8 to 10 minutes. Dry and freeze leftovers.

ABOUT SHERRI

A reformed pessimist and a recent hopeful romantic, **SHERRI SHACKELFORD** writes lively and heartwarming stories, featuring rugged cowboys, for Harlequin Love Inspired Historical. Her books are available from Amazon, Barnes & Noble, Harlequin and most major retailers. Stay in contact with Sherri through her web site at sherrishackelford.com, on Facebook or email at sherrishackelford@gmail.com.

RESCUING LEEDA

BY CAROLYNE AARSEN

Of course this would happen now.

Leeda lifted the hood of the car, coughing as antifreeze-laden clouds billowed out of the engine. Seriously? On the one day she was determined to make a good impression? She glared at her uncooperative car with antifreeze puddling on the pavement and the engine hissing and ticking as it cooled. She imagined the dish she was bringing to the potluck cooling as well.

"'Go to the potluck at the church. Maybe you'll meet somebody,'" she said, mimicking her aunt's sweet voice as she walked around the car to check on her food, her steps wobbly in her high heels.

This was phase two of her good impression, along with the demure skirt and shirt her aunt, in whose basement she resided, helped her choose. So far her mother's advice to return to the town they'd once lived in had been anything but helpful, and her aunt's promise that everything would be all right wasn't working out so well either. Her job search hadn't produced a single lead yet, and now her car was dead.

Thankfully, the pot holding her chicken was still warm, at least for a little while. Leeda wrapped it up again, glancing desperately down the road. She wasn't the praying sort. She left that up to her mother – her father, too, when he was alive – but right about now it couldn't hurt.

"A little bit of help here, Lord," she whispered, wrapping her sweater around her shoulders. "A little nudge to let me know you're watching over me like Mom and Dad always said you were."

She waited, listening, then snorted. Typical. God hadn't helped her when she'd lost her job and her apartment back in Toronto. Why would He help her out here?

And just then she heard the faint growl of a truck engine. Soon a pickup crested the hill. Hope bloomed in her chest as the truck slowed and coasted to a stop behind her car. A man got out, and Leeda's hope was tempered with a dose of common sense. She was all alone.

But this guy wore his hair neatly clipped, his blue jeans were faded just enough, his cowboy boots were slightly scuffed, and his crisp white shirt was rolled up over his elbows. Not your typical axe-murderer outfit. But then Leeda wasn't sure she was any judge of character. Case in point, Jax, her very ex-boyfriend.

"You got some trouble here?" the man asked, striding toward her with that rolling gait typical of cowboys.

"Yeah. Radiator and rocks. Not a good combination." She poked her thumb over her shoulder at her disabled car.

"I see that."

He gave her a warm smile that created a fan of wrinkles around his chocolate-brown eyes. In spite of her previous concerns, she sighed inwardly. He seemed really nice.

"Can I just have a quick look?" he asked, his smile creating another flutter.

"Knock yourself out. Just watch the hood support. If it gives way, you might, literally, knock yourself out."

His crooked grin made her want to do a facepalm.

Seriously. That mouth.

He did a quick inspection, crouching down to look at the engine from another angle, then closed the hood with a clang. "You're right. Bad combo. I'm going out on a limb here and guessing you need a ride."

"I do." She narrowed her eyes. "You're not wanted for any criminal act, are you? Like murder maybe?"

"I do have an outstanding parking ticket I hope to square up soon."

"Sounds sketchy, but I think I can let that slide. Given that it doesn't seem like anyone else is coming by out here. And my Parmesan chicken is getting cooler by the minute."

"You going to the potluck at the church?"

He knew about the potluck? Was he *going* to the potluck? Her aunt wasn't kidding when she'd said there would be handsome guys there. "Uh. Well, I was. I was taking the pot and was about to give up on the *luck*, but now that you're here…"

"It's your lucky day."

Seriously, that smile should have been illegal.

"I'll just get my chicken."

She took the box holding her casserole dish out of the backseat of her car, then grabbed her purse from the front seat, but before closing the door, she took a moment to center herself. *Don't get pulled in by charm and good looks again. You're just getting a ride from him.* He probably had a girlfriend in every stop on the rodeo circuit, anyway.

Then she turned, and he was right next to her, holding out his hands. "Here, let me take that, ma'am."

Leeda couldn't remember the last time she'd been *ma'amed*. And when his rough hands brushed hers and their gazes tangled, she momentarily forgot her little self-talk. "Sure. I hope it will stay warm 'til we get there."

"There's a couple of microwaves in the kitchen you can use to heat it up," her rescuer said. "But before we venture on this new phase of our relationship, I should introduce myself. I'm Chuck."

133

"Leeda. Leeda Vandekeere." As soon as she gave her last name, she realized he hadn't extended the same courtesy.

"Of the Holmes Crossing Vandekeeres?" he asked as he opened the door for her.

"Yes. My father was from here." Getting in the car, she reached out her hands for the box. "I moved here from Toronto a week ago."

"Pastor VandeKeere was a good man." He gently rested the package in her arms.

The reverence with which he spoke her father's name, plus the fact that he knew her father was a preacher, eased away the rest of her misgivings. Besides what self-respecting serial killer would know that there were two microwaves in the church kitchen?

"Did you know my father when he was a pastor here?" Leeda set her purse on the floor of the truck. A clean floor, she noticed.

"No. He was before my time, but I've heard a lot about him. He had a good reputation. A very powerful preacher, I was told."

"He was." Leeda felt a flush of guilt that she couldn't join in the admiration. She'd loved her father, but his high expectations and her lifestyle never truly meshed. She was always pushing, and he was always pulling her back.

"You sound hesitant."

"If you know about my dad, then you probably also know that I was the typical Preacher's Kid. The rebel."

"Can't say as I've heard much about that." His smile was as broad as ever. "But that doesn't matter. Reputations, like resolutions, are made to be broken."

"Well, there's one resolution I won't break, and that's to stay as far away from pastors as possible. In any way, shape or form."

"So I'm guessing your boyfriend isn't a pastor."

"No boyfriend at all, but if I was looking – and I'm not – I wouldn't be looking at pastors."

"I see" was all Chuck said as he started the truck up with a roar. He gave her an apologetic look as he pulled onto the road. "Sorry. Older truck. Noisy diesel engine."

"No judging here. At least yours starts."

He laughed at that and turned on the radio, classical music coming through the speakers. Another pleasant surprise.

"Not gonna lie, I was expecting to hear Keith Urban or Taylor Swift."

"Don't let anyone in Holmes Crossing know," he said in a mock whisper, "but I don't really like country music."

"Color me shocked." Leeda faked a horrified look. "And what does your girlfriend think of that?"

Uh-oh. Clunker. Clumsy.

But it was out there now.

"Very smooth," he said, causing her to flush. He was onto her. "But no girlfriend. And you, I understand, don't have a boyfriend."

"Nope. Nobody."

"Well, that's convenient. So how did you hear about the potluck?"

"My aunt told me." A tiny shiver of expectation filled her as Chuck glanced at her sidelong and caught her staring. "She suggested I go."

"I'm glad she did." Another killer smile. "So what do you do?"

"So far, I help my aunt clean her chicken coop, weed the garden and apply for jobs. Not exactly living the dream I expected when I moved here from out East."

"What did you do before you came?"

"Worked as an administrative assistant, which, let's face it, is a glorified way to say secretary."

"You any good?"

As Chuck's gaze flicked again from the road to her, the sparkle in his eyes hinted that he was teasing. It also made her heart flutter a bit more.

"I can multi-task like a banshee." She dragged her gaze away from him, watching the road ahead, edged by trees and open fields as darker memories of her previous job and boss

135

edged into the sunny day.

"You look sad."

Leeda shrugged. "Just old stuff."

"Old boyfriends?"

"No. My old boss was not . . . not . . . " She hesitated, unsure she wanted to lay bare the mess that sent her fleeing from Toronto.

"Not a good man, I'm guessing."

The hard edge in his voice and the grim set of his jaw created an initial flicker of fear in Leeda, but when he looked at her, the warmth of his gaze made her feel oddly safe.

"That's too bad," he said. "Not all bosses are bad."

"I know that. I liked the job. I just didn't like the atmosphere and, quite honestly, the city either."

"And you like it out here?"

Leeda glanced out the window, smiling. The crops in the fields were just changing color, a harbinger of the harvest season she remembered from her childhood. She released a long, slow breath of gratitude. "I really do."

"Well, if you're going to be staying awhile, I know of a secretarial job, if you're interested. The boss is a decent guy. I can personally vouch for him."

Her head spun back so quickly she almost blinded herself by her flying hair. "Really? Doing what?"

"Church secretary."

"Working for the pastor?"

"I know you wanted to stay away from pastors, but he's not bad. For a preacher."

She shrugged. "I didn't say I couldn't work for one. I just couldn't date one."

"Because of your dad?" he wanted to know.

"I wasn't a good preacher's daughter. I doubt I would make a good preacher's wife."

"I think you should let God be the judge of how good you can be at what you do," he said as they rattled across a metal bridge, a train trestle beside it. "He knows your heart, and I'm going to go out on a limb and say it's a good one."

136

His words seemed to soothe a restlessness she'd felt the past few years, and if she wasn't careful, she might just believe him. "You don't know that."

"I know that you're willing to attend a potluck at a church on a Friday night. You could be over there." He angled his chin toward the hotel with attached bar that they passed before turning onto Main Street.

"Not my idea of fun."

"See? A good heart."

"I see the steeple of the church," she said quietly as they drove down Main Street with its mixture of brick buildings and Stucco false fronts.

"You still attend?"

"I haven't since I've been here, but I want to." She gave him an impish smile, surprised at the warmth in the smile he returned. "Do you go?"

"Pretty regularly."

She looked at him and took a chance as they came closer to the church. For some reason, she had a panicky feeling that she had to do something slightly outrageous before they stopped. Before they ended up surrounded by other people. Before she lost her nerve.

"Would you be willing to pick me up on Sunday?" she asked, hoping she sounded casual. Innocent. "My car is, obviously, out of commission."

"I'd love to. Maybe we could do lunch afterwards." He parked the truck and gave her a broad smile that held a hint of promise.

"I'd like that."

The kitchen was bustling with activity, women calling out for serving spoons, heat emanating from the stove and mouth-watering scents braiding around each other. A sense of homecoming filled her as they stepped inside.

Chuck set her dish by the microwave. "If you need to heat it up, you can use this one."

"Thanks so much."

"I've gotta arrange a few things." He scratched his chin

with a forefinger. "You'll still be here?"

The warmth in his voice gave her a tingle up her back. "Of course."

He held her gaze a beat longer than necessary, and then he put his hand on her shoulder, giving it a light squeeze. Her breath quickened.

"There you are, Pastor Charles," a woman called out, walking over to Chuck and Leeda. "I was hoping you could open the supper in prayer."

Leeda could only stare at "Chuck," guessing he was the "Pastor Charles" her aunt had been raving about ever since she'd arrived.

"You said you'd still be here," he said, his voice lowering, just for her.

She hesitated, but when her gaze met his, she felt it again. That curious sense of homecoming. Of belonging.

"I look forward to your prayer," she said, touching his hand with hers.

A small connection. A gentle bond.

Her aunt was right, she thought, as she turned to put the chicken in the microwave.

She had a feeling it would all be just fine.

A NOTE FROM CAROLYNE

This recipe was given to me by my brother, who made it up. I don't measure the ingredients, so I had to wing it a bit to get the proportions right. You might want to adjust according to your own tastes. It's a lovely combination of flavors and a way to dress up chicken breasts for a "company dinner."

PARMESAN CHICKEN

2 chicken breasts
½ cup flour
1½ teaspoons seasoning salt
2 eggs
2 tablespoons butter
1/3 cup Parmesan cheese
½ teaspoon basil
½ teaspoon oregano
¼ teaspoon black pepper
¼-½ teaspoon garlic powder

Blend flour and seasoning salt. Set aside. Mix eggs, Parmesan, basil, oregano and pepper. Set aside. Heat butter and garlic powder in frying pan until brown. Drench chicken in flour/seasoning salt mixture. Thoroughly coat in the egg/Parmesan mixture and let drip to remove excess. Brown in frying pan a couple of minutes on each side to set mixture. Remove from pan. Bake on cookie sheet for 30 minutes at 350 degrees.

ABOUT CAROLYNE

CAROLYNE AARSEN lives in Alberta, Canada, at the intersection of *No* and *Where* with one husband, one dog, nine horses and endless fields. When her kids left, she gained time to be involved in her church and puzzle out stories on long walks. She is thankful to write for Love Inspired and enjoys receiving reader letters. Sign up for the newsletter on her web page, www.carolyneaarsen.com, to stay in the know.

HOMECOMING

BY DEBBY GIUSTI

Martha Jane "Marti" Baker hadn't been behind the wheel of a car since her Aunt Libby's funeral almost a year earlier. Living in New York City, she didn't need private transportation, but flying to Atlanta and heading south to Sweetgum, Georgia, required renting a car and navigating the back roads. She glanced at her watch, grateful to be ahead of schedule. When she'd made her travel plans to meet the real-estate agent, she hadn't expected the October storm and pounding rain.

Turning the wipers to high, Marti peered through the downpour. Hopefully, the deluge would ease before she arrived at Aunt Libby's house. The memory of the loving woman who'd raised her brought a swell of grief. Marti should have returned to Sweetgum after college, instead of fleeing north, but at the time, she'd needed to find herself. She'd found many things in New York, but not the love and acceptance Aunt Libby had so freely given.

Unexpected tears spilled from her eyes. She swiped her hand across her cheeks and startled as a car horn sounded.

From out of nowhere, an orange pickup flew around her, nearly sideswiping the rental car. In an attempt to avoid a crash, Marti turned the wheel. The car hydroplaned on the slick road and skidded over the shoulder into the ditch.

She screamed. Her head flew back against the seat as the car came to a rest. For a moment, she lost sense of time before the hammering rain brought her back to the present. Digging into her handbag, she found her cell and tapped in 911, then sighed with frustration when the call failed.

Needing to assess the damage, she thrust open the car door. Chilling rain lashed at her face as she stepped onto the soggy ground and stared into the distance where the menacing pickup had disappeared.

I haven't given you much time over the last few years, God, but Aunt Libby always said you were close at hand. That's what I need now, a helping hand.

"You okay?" a voice called from a small dirt path.

She squinted at the man in a camouflage slicker walking toward her with a very decided limp. Hopefully he was friend, not foe.

"An orange pickup ran me off the road."

"Did you get the license-plate number?"

"It happened too fast." She held up her cell. "I can't get my phone to work."

"Coverage is spotty this far from town." The guy approached, looking big and bulky under the camo covering.

Something about his eyes brought back memories from her youth. Reluctant to accept what her mind was telling her, Marti took a step back.

He hitched a thumb over his shoulder. "You're welcome to use my landline. My cabin's just behind that clump of pines." He hesitated a moment as if assessing her concern before he extended his hand. "Carl Evans."

His grip was strong, decisive. A shiver of realization stirred within her. She was surprised she hadn't recognized him immediately, but the limp had thrown her off.

"Thanks." She waited as the rain soaked her hair, until it

143

became evident that *he* hadn't remembered *her*. "I'm Marti."

"You need to get out of this weather," he said simply. "I've got hot coffee and a blazing fire to warm you while I tow your car out of the ditch and change your tire."

She followed his gaze and, for the first time, noticed the flat. Groaning, she turned back to the deep-set eyes and full lips that had filled too many of her teenage daydreams. Carlson Evans had been the high school jock every girl wanted to date. Marti had succumbed to his charm, but he and his friend, Grant, never had eyes for a skinny girl with buckteeth and glasses. Funny how she'd let the captain of the football team and cross-country star influence her own self-worth.

She shivered as a stiff wind tangled with the rain and her memory. "I appreciate the offer. I'll take you up on the coffee, but I'll need to call the rental-car company and then a tow truck."

He laughed as he directed her along the path. "We're eight miles from town. Smiley's Tow Service is slow at best, and it's the only one around. And there's probably not enough damage to bother calling the rental company. Might as well accept my help. After six years in the military, I know a few things about automotive repair."

He shrugged out of his slicker and wrapped it around her shoulders, pulling the hood up over her head. Surprised by his thoughtfulness, she fell into step beside him, but even with his lopsided gait, Marti was hard-pressed to keep up. As much as she wanted to know about his injury, she wouldn't pry.

The rugged A-frame came into view. The wrap-around porch and welcoming rocking chair drove away any reservation she might have had about following him inside. The smell of freshly brewed coffee greeted them, mixed with the tangy scent of onions and garlic that made her mouth water and reminded her that she'd skipped breakfast in the hurry to catch her flight and hadn't stopped to eat since.

Carlson helped her out of the raincoat, hung it on a hook by the door and ushered her to the fireplace. As she shook rain from her hair and stretched her hands toward the warmth, he moved into the small but tidy kitchen. "Coffee?"

"Sounds good. Black with a little milk." He fixed her a cup and poured one for himself.

Accepting the mug, she raised it to her lips, appreciating the hearty brew that displaced the chill. "You mentioned the military. Are you still on active duty?"

He returned to the stove and lifted the lid off a stoneware pot. "I came home to Sweetgum about nine months ago."

"Things have changed?" she asked.

He shrugged. "Maybe. But I've changed most of all."

Grabbing a wooden spoon from a nearby drawer, he stirred the pot. "Chili's almost done. Have you had lunch?"

She glanced at her watch. One-fifteen. "Thanks, but I'm supposed to meet someone in an hour. I flew in today from New York for this meeting."

"Then I'd better change that tire. Drink your coffee and dry out in here. Won't take me long."

Before she could object, he'd exited the cabin, leaving her to wonder how and why she'd ended up in the ditch in his front yard. If Aunt Libby were still alive, Marti would blame her for stirring up trouble.

With a sigh, she settled into an overstuffed chair, positioned close to the fireplace, and placed the mug on a side table next to a dog-eared Bible. Touching the soft leather cover, she closed her eyes, thinking of her restless night and early-morning flight. Her mind drifted back to her youth. Carlson was staring at her from his locker and turned to catch her arm as she walked by . . .

Her eyes flew open, ending the dream and putting her face-to-face with an older and – could it be – more handsome version of his teenage self.

"Your car's ready."

She blinked, seeing the tiny lines around his eyes and the wide smile that made her heart pound. "I . . . I drifted off."

"You were talking in your sleep. Something about prom."

She straightened her dress. "I didn't go to prom."

He shrugged. "It's overrated."

"Tell that to a seventeen year old without a date."

Tilting his head, he stared at her for a long moment.

Frustrated that he still hadn't recognized her, she reached for her purse and stood. "I need to pay you."

Confusion washed over his face. He held up his hand. "That's one way to insult a person around these parts. Help's freely given in Sweetgum."

"Then thanks for your help."

He tugged at his jaw. "You know it probably sounds strange, but you look familiar."

No reason not to be truthful. "Sweetgum High."

His eyes widened. "Jane? Martha Jane Baker?"

"'Plain Jane' as you and your sidekick, Grant, used to call me."

Carlson shook his head. "I never said that about you."

"Really? You laughed enough times when he taunted me."

"Teased, maybe, but never taunted."

"Evidently your memory differs from mine." Steeling her shoulders, she shoved past him and opened the front door. "I'm sure you and Grant will have a good laugh on me when you get together." Stepping onto the porch, she glanced back.

"Grant died." The somberness of Carlson's words cut into her heart. "We were on patrol in Afghanistan. I couldn't save him."

"I. . . I'm sorry." The door swung closed, shutting her out.

Tears stung her eyes, and his words muddled her thoughts as she hurried to the car and climbed behind the wheel. Why couldn't she forgive and forget? Hadn't she gone to New York to leave "Plain Jane" behind? Braces, contacts and Pilates had worked to her advantage, but no matter the outer trappings, she was still that same confused teenager inside. She needed to go back to New York and pretend to be the pretty girl with straight teeth and stylish clothes and leave Carlson and her painful memories where they belonged. In the past.

Carl swallowed back the memory of the IED explosion and his long road to recovery. He'd survived when Grant hadn't, a

146

heavy weight to carry.

Jane Baker – or "Marti" as she called herself now – seemed to have scars from the past as well. Growing up, she'd lived in a big country house, filled with expensive antiques, and never had time for a guy without money or privilege. A guy who needed the military to make him a man.

God, you've got an ironic sense of timing. Carl carried her mug to the sink. His cell rang before he could place it in the dishwasher.

"Deputy Evans?" The dispatcher's voice was tense with concern. "I know you're off-duty, but the sheriff wanted me to notify you. The Pine Ridge Bank was robbed. Lone gunman. Six-two, two-ten, wearing green-flannel shirt and jeans."

"Sounds like the same guy who robbed the other two banks."

"Except this time someone spotted him driving away in an orange Ford 4 X 4."

Carl reached for his holster and strapped on his weapon. "An orange pickup ran someone off Pike's Road near my cabin. Tell Sheriff Knolls the vehicle headed west."

"Toward Libby Baker's old place?"

His heart lunged. Was that where Jane was going?

"I'm driving there now. Send backup."

The ride to the Baker home took longer than Carl had expected. He parked in the woods and hurried on foot toward the barn and glanced inside. His chest constricted, seeing the pickup. Fearing the worst, he edged toward the house and peered through a side window. Marti sat in a chair, her arms tied behind her back. A beefy guy holding a Glock stood nearby. Carl climbed the back steps and reached for the doorknob. Drawing his weapon, he stepped into the kitchen.

"Some gal found me in the old house," a male voice said, the sound coming from the living room. "I'll leave here tonight after I kill her."

"You'll never get away with it," Marti cried out.

"Shut up, or I'll tape your mouth."

"I'm expecting someone," she said. "A real-estate agent."

"Then I'll kill her, too."

Carl eased open the door that led from the kitchen to the living area.

The guy's back was to the door. He held a phone to his ear. "Another heist tomorrow and then I'm done."

A floorboard creaked. The gunman turned and raised his weapon.

Carl fired.

The guy wheezed, dropped to his knees and collapsed unconscious onto the floor.

Marti screamed.

He cuffed the gunman, then reached for her. "You're safe. I've got you." He cut the ties binding her hands and pulled her close. Sirens sounded in the distance.

"He was . . . in . . . the house," she gasped. "I didn't expect to find . . . anyone."

"Did he hurt you?"

She shook her head. "I'm alright."

In a scurry of activity, Sheriff Knowles and the on-duty deputies swarmed the house and took the robber away by ambulance.

Once the excitement subsided, Carl turned to Marti. "Are you sure you're okay?"

She nodded. "But I'm sorry about Grant."

"Grant and I had a lot to learn."

"Maybe I was too sensitive. I was trying to find myself."

"You seemed independent to me, which is a good thing. I was always following Grant's lead. When I was recuperating after my foot was amputated—"

Her eyes widened. "I didn't know."

"No more long-distance races, but thanks to an artificial foot and a great team of surgeons, I can still get around."

One of the sheriff's deputies hurried inside. "A real-estate agent is asking for you, ma'am. She's got someone who wants to buy your aunt's house."

Carl's heart stopped. "You're going back to New York?"

"Tomorrow."

He let out a stiff breath and glanced at the high ceilings and crown molding. "Seems a shame to sell a beautiful house like this."

"It needs repair."

"I know a former military guy who likes to work with his hands."

"Really?" Hesitating for only a heartbeat, she turned to the deputy. "Tell the real estate agent I'm not ready to sell."

Carl slipped his hand into hers as the deputy hurried away. "The chili's still hot. After the sheriff and his men finish here, why don't you come over for lunch?"

"Lunch sounds perfect."

"Then you're staying in Sweetgum?"

"Actually, I don't know why I left."

"Welcome home, Marti."

She pulled him close and stretched to kiss his cheek. "For old times' sake, why don't you call me Jane?"

A NOTE FROM DEBBY

I hope you enjoy my Mother's chili recipe that always reminds me of home. This is great comfort food that's especially good on a cold day.

HOMECOMING CHILI

1 ½ pounds ground chuck
2 cloves garlic
2 (28-ounce) cans whole tomatoes
1 (15-ounce) can red kidney beans (drained)
1 (15-ounce) can diced tomatoes (basil, oregano)
1 large sweet onion
1 (15-ounce) can tomato sauce
1 (15-ounce) can black beans (drained)
1 (15-ounce) can whole kernel corn
1 (6-ounce) can tomato paste
Seasonings to taste: chili powder, cayenne pepper, cumin, salt, black pepper

Sauté diced onion and garlic in oil. Add ground chuck and seasonings. Once meat is browned, add vegetables. Simmer for two hours. Serve plain or over rice and topped with shredded cheddar cheese.

ABOUT DEBBY

DEBBY GIUSTI is an award-winning Christian author who met and married her husband – then a Captain in the Army – at Fort Knox, Kentucky. Together they traveled the world, raised three wonderful children and have now settled in Atlanta, Georgia, where Debby spins tales of mystery and suspense that touch the heart and soul. Visit Debby online at www.DebbyGiusti.com, www.seekerville.blogspot.com and www.craftieladiesofromance.blogspot.com and email her at Debby@DebbyGiusti.com.

FOOTPRINTS IN THE SNOW

BY PAMELA TRACY

A puzzle depicting Santa Claus and Rudolf, halfway complete, took up most of the kitchen table. Its pieces were no longer sorted, and Angela Vermeer was pretty sure the cat had played soccer with one corner section.

"Mom, will Santa bring me the Death Star? I want it more than anything. I was good enough, wasn't I?"

"Go to bed," Angela said, putting her cup of hot chocolate on the counter. Danny, the youngest, had already fallen asleep on the top bunk bed. Now, it was after ten, and she'd already guided Jacob, her oldest, to bed three times. "Santa can't come if you're awake."

Jacob, all mussy brown hair and reindeer pajamas, still believed in Santa, although he'd already denied the tooth fairy and the Easter Bunny.

"Come sleep with me. Please." He half-danced toward his bedroom.

"I can't."

The dance ended, the smile faded, and Jacob shuffled back

to bed. Torn, Angela shot a guilty look at the table. On the other end were the remnants of their traditional Christmas Eve dinner, four hours old.

Spaghetti.

Captain Jackson Carpenter had laughed last Christmas Eve when she'd served it. She'd met him at an air show six months before that while he was stationed at Offutt Air Force Base, not far from her home in Omaha, Nebraska. She'd escorted two of her students to the show, and he was one of the men of the 55th Wing who'd answered questions about the A-10 Thunderbolt. She'd been impressed by the terms "loiter times" and "wide combat radius." He'd been impressed by her long dark hair and even darker eyes.

She'd planned to brush him off when he'd asked for her phone number, but her favorite third grader, a Down Syndrome angel, thickly said, "Mrs. Verma, give to him. He a soldier."

To her surprise, Jackson had called the next day, a century before she'd been ready to date again. So, she'd mentioned having two children, ages six and eight. Instead of making an excuse to hang up, he'd said, "I have six brothers." When she mentioned going to church, he'd told her where he attended, adding, "I only miss when I'm on duty." She'd thought of a dozen reasons to turn him down but figured one date would do the trick.

They'd started with dinner and a movie.

And, she'd laughed the whole night. The man put ketchup on everything, even Mexican food. She'd never been around an enlisted man before. Jackson had stories and songs unending. Right in the restaurant, he'd sung to her about the biscuits in the Army in the song, "Gee, Mom, I Wanna Go Home."

He'd met the boys after their third date, her parents after their sixth, and he'd started attending her church after their tenth date.

She hadn't met his parents yet because Florida was so far from Nebraska. But they'd sounded nice on the phone. "Call me Rosemary," his mother had insisted. "You're all he talks about lately."

That was when Angela had suspected that maybe Jackson could be more than a friend.

Her sons, though, hadn't warmed to him. They'd said Jackson was coming over too often, taking up her time. Never mind that he knew all the names of Thomas the Train's friends. Never mind that he'd actually once built the Death Star out of Legos.

Last month Jackson had discussed the Christmas gift he would get them. She'd advised him not to spend more than he should, not to try to buy their affection. All that mattered, she'd emphasized, was showing them that he cared. Up until last week, she'd been wondering what he'd decided on. Now, she wondered if she would find out at all.

She hadn't heard from him in a week.

Angela picked up the bowl of sauce, empty except for a few dried smears, and remembered their last Christmas.

"Spaghetti? Really? For Christmas Eve?" Then, Jackson had tasted the homemade sauce and the hand-rolled meatballs and stated, "I want this every year."

"It's my Aunt Stacey's recipe," Angela had told him. "She always claimed it made the world better."

It hadn't tonight.

Two months ago Jackson had been sent to Afghanistan. At first, he'd emailed her every day and called at least once a week. He hadn't talked much about what was happening there.

"When will you be home?" she'd kept asking.

"Soon," he'd promised.

In the last three days, she'd called his mom twice, only to be told, "I'm sure he's just busy." Then, Rosemary had gone on to talk about his brothers.

Unfulfilled . . . that's how Angela had felt after hanging up the phone. Something was missing. She'd gotten used to Jackson's presence, his reassuring voice.

Today she'd made enough spaghetti to feed the entire 55th Wing. Now, she needed to clear the plates, scrub the table and decorate it with the Christmas tablecloth. She would add red candles and center a dish of Christmas cookies between them.

"Mom." Jacob had returned. "I'm so tired."

So was she.

Bending down to hug him, she said, "I'll come with you. Go get under the covers. Let me do a few things first."

"But I can't sleep. Come now. Pleeeasse." Of her two sons, Jacob was the worrier. He checked his backpack twice to make sure he had his lunchbox. He checked his Pokemon cards daily to make sure none had slipped from their pockets and fallen under the couch. At night, his bedroom door had to stay open.

Angela held on tight to Jacob, enjoying the little-boy smell that never went away, even after being drenched in Scooby Doo shampoo and soap. She figured Jacob worried so because he remembered his father. Thomas Vermeer had left for work one Friday morning four years ago and had never returned. A three-car pileup on Interstate Forty, just north of Grand Island, had ended a strong ten-year marriage and left two little boys standing at the door waiting for Daddy.

"A watched pot never boils," Angela had told Jacob over and over on that day that neither she nor her son would ever forget. Now she needed to tell herself the same thing. There had to be a reason for Jackson's silence. Either he'd been too busy – please, God – or he'd forgotten about her – please, no, God – or . . . No, not that.

"I'm going to make a phone call, and then I'll lie down with you," she told Jacob.

"And play video games?"

"No, not when Santa will be here in just a few hours."

"Can we play tickle monster?"

She smiled. "That we can do. For one minute."

As he danced off to bed, relief washed away the pinched look on his face. No ten year old should worry this much.

Then I have to stop worrying, she scolded herself. Angela sat on the couch in the living room. The tree, with sparkling lights and mostly homemade decorations, stood in the corner, next to the window that showcased a snow-covered front yard. Beneath the tree were a few presents. When the boys fell asleep – make that when Jacob finally fell asleep – she could take out the ones labeled *FROM SANTA.*

She took her cell phone from the coffee table. Jackson had been calling her from a phone center. He got what was called a fifteen-minute morale call. She could certainly use a little morale boost right now.

Because of where Jackson was and what he was doing, his phone would most likely be set to vibrate, but that didn't mean a soldier wanted to be interrupted during a dangerous situation. She'd called two days ago and had left a message, but she hadn't received a call back.

Who could she call here in the states?

She hadn't met his commander, and while she'd met a few of his buddies, she didn't know their phone numbers. Besides, she didn't want to seem like someone who clung too tightly.

Angela returned the phone to the coffee table, closed the curtains and crawled into Jacob's bunk to play tickle monster for a whole minute. Danny was still asleep on the top bunk. Only a thunderstorm would wake him. Nothing else did, not loud television, a video game or tickle monster.

"Mom," Jacob said when things had quieted, "what if Santa accidentally forgets—"

"Shhh," Angela soothed. "He won't."

And, while she said the words, she was thinking, *God doesn't accidentally forget his children's wants or needs.*

It only took a few minutes, as Jacob told her again what he wanted for Christmas, before he turned over and fell asleep. She'd intended to head for the living room and start getting things ready. Instead, she fell asleep, watching the rise and fall of her son's chest.

It felt like a minute. Really, it had been five hours, if the glowing orange numbers on Yoda's stomach clock were correct. Beside her, Jacob snored. Outside, something clunked. *Clunk. Clunk.* She sat up and was already in the living room when the next sound came.

It started as a clunk but ended with a crash against the side of the house. She snatched her phone from the coffee table and stood by the front door, listening. The tree in the front yard was old. Maybe a branch? But the first sounds had come from the roof.

It was dark, but the moon was doing its job of lighting the way. Stepping to the window, she waited a moment before brushing aside the curtain.

"Ahhhhhhhh."

Someone was hurt outside her window.

The next "Ohhhhhhhhh" sounded familiar.

She flipped on the porch light and opened the curtains wide enough to peek out. A strange, bulky heap was on top of the bush next to the house. A man lay there, half-covered by snow, one red-covered leg thrust in the air, his foot tangled in the gutter that had been attached to her roof.

He wasn't moving, not even the red hat with the white pom-pom. No way was Angela calling 911 on Santa! Angela bustled out the door and to the bush, stopping a few feet away in amazement.

Jackson Carpenter both moaned and grinned at her. "I was hoping for a bit more romantic greeting."

She eyed his predicament.

"My leg is caught. And I think I ripped my pants."

"Jackson! What were you doing on my roof? Why didn't you call first?" The words came out in bursts – fear, amazement, joy – as she hurried to him, not caring about the cold snow. "Oh, I'm sooo glad you're home."

Home? Until then she hadn't admitted, even to herself, how much she longed to build a life with Jackson.

He sat up, clutching her to him even as Angela, ever practical, reached up to try to disconnect his ripped pant leg that was caught on the broken gutter. It had both stopped his fall and trapped him.

"Some things are more important." He put his gloved hands on her cold cheeks, drew her forward and gave her the kind of kiss that melted snow.

She gave up on trying to reach the gutter. When the cold could no longer be ignored, she helped him take off the bottom of his Santa suit. Then, Jackson, long-john bottoms gleaming like snow from beneath his bright red jacket, hurried into the house and to the bathroom while Angela untangled his pants. She stepped to her sidewalk so she could look at the roof where Jackson, with a shovel and giant fake reindeer hoof, had made footprints in the snow.

"So the kids would think Santa had really been here," he said a few minutes later, as he sat in his torn Santa pants, sipping hot chocolate and eating leftover spaghetti and meatballs. "I was trying to time it so they'd even get a glimpse of me in the front yard."

"Why didn't you tell me you were coming home?" Angela asked. "It was a great idea. I would have helped."

"Well," Jackson said, "I was hoping to get a few things done to surprise you. But, since you're awake . . ."

Something in the way Jackson looked at her made her breath catch. He held out his hand, revealing a tiny, velvet box, the same color as his Santa suit.

"Yes," she whispered, without reaching for the box.

He opened it himself, withdrawing a ring she didn't even look at. She was too busy staring at him.

"You did surprised me."

"Can I surprise you forever?" he asked, slipping the ring on her finger.

Before she could answer, Jacob's voice came from the kitchen doorway.

"You made Mommy smile again." Jacob spoke, but Danny stood next to him, nodding.

"I can do that for you, too," Jackson said. Taking the boys' hands, never mind that they were in their pajamas and he in a ripped Santa suit, he led them outside where they could see the reindeer footprints on the roof.

From the living room window, Angela watched them, feeling settled, and then she looked down at the ring on her finger.

Forever.

159

A NOTE FROM PAMELA

I've written many books in my career, and one of the reasons I've been able to do that is that I don't really cook. One of my best friends, Stacey Rannik, has made it a goal to change this "flaw." This is Stacey's recipe, one of my favorites. If I wanted to start cooking – and I might someday – I would make this recipe first.

AUNT STACEY'S SPAGHETTI & MEATBALLS

Sauce:

6 cloves garlic
1 large onion, chopped
3 tablespoons olive oil
1 (6-ounce) can tomato paste
1 (8-ounce) can tomato sauce
2 (16-ounce) cans tomatoes
1 package baby Bella mushrooms (sliced)
2 teaspoons sugar
2 cups water
½ cup fresh parsley (chopped)
2 bay leaves
1 teaspoon fresh rosemary (chopped)
1 teaspoon each (basil, thyme, oregano, pepper, salt)

In a large Dutch oven, cook garlic and onions in oil until golden. Add remaining ingredients. Cover and simmer gently for two hours or longer.

Meatballs:

1 pound ground beef
1 pound ground pork
4 tablespoons chopped onion
4 tablespoons chopped celery leaves
¾ cup bread crumbs
¾ cup milk
2 eggs
2 garlic cloves, minced
1 teaspoon salt
1 teaspoon pepper
½ cup grated fresh Parmesan
 * Optional (add Tabasco or Worcestershire Sauce to taste)

Combine all ingredients. Shape into balls. Brown in a hot skillet. Add to sauce and simmer for 30 minutes or longer. Serve over spaghetti.

ABOUT PAMELA

PAMELA TRACY is an award-winning author of 27 novels, with more than 1 million books in print. She lives with her husband and son in central Nebraska. Her 2007 suspense, *Pursuit of Justice*, was a Romance Writers of America RITA finalist, and her 2009 suspense, *Broken Lullaby*, won the American Christian Fiction Writers' Book of the Year award. Stay in contact with Pamela through her web site at www.pamelatracy.com.

DESSERTS/TREATS

A TASTE OF CHRISTMAS

BY LENORA WORTH

"Well, you know the bread's the most important part."

"Really now?" Brice Taylor grinned over at the woman he'd known all his life. "And since when did little Alice Whitman learn to make bread pudding? Amaretto Bread Pudding, at that?"

Alice gave him that impish smile he remembered so well. Except now, it was also a mature, feminine smile from a woman who lived and worked in New Orleans. "Since I grew up and went to work for a cooking show on the Let's Eat Network."

Brice nabbed a slice of day-old French bread, real admiration beneath his teasing smile. "Oh, right. I seem to recall—"

"Of course, you recall." She slapped at his hand. "My mom only tells anyone who will listen that her smart, cute daughter works in production for that good-looking chef, Remy Carrell, and that I bring home samples every time I come to visit."

"Which is apparently rare from what your brother tells me," Brice said. "In fact, I'm surprised his long-lost sister made it back to Atlanta for his wedding."

"I'm not that far from Atlanta." Alice's pout showed through her dimples. "I get home when I can."

Brice held up his hands. "Hey, not judging. I live closer than you do, and I don't visit my parents as much as my mom would like. She reminds me of that every time I do come for holidays or long weekends."

"I guess writing and recording with some of the biggest names in music gives you a good excuse to stay in Memphis."

He lifted a brow. "And cooking good food sure gives you an excuse to take it easy in the Big Easy."

"Okay, so we're both on the naughty list this year," Alice said. "It's just that I really love my job, and taping the show takes up a lot of time and energy. What can I say? I like making a living at something I never dreamed I'd wind up doing." She turned on the oven, her long ponytail swinging over her shoulder. "New Orleans is an amazing place full of interesting people who love good food. Keeps all of us hopping."

"So you love living in Louisiana?" Brice asked, already knowing the answer. "You've been there for five years now. Not counting the four years you were away at college, of course."

"Are you counting?" she shot back, her fingers tearing into the stale bread with gusto. "Hey, do you want to learn how to make bread pudding or not?"

"You mean 'Christmas Bread Pudding with Amaretto Sauce,'" he read off the recipe page. "Pecans, cherries, coconut. Did you throw in the kitchen sink, too?"

"Everything but that, I guess. It's my own special recipe."

"I want to learn how to make it, all right, but I especially want to practice eating it," Brice said. "I didn't get up early just to admire your mom's Christmas decorations. I want to be a master bread-pudding cooker."

"Well, when you put it that way. . . I'm honored you deemed me worthy of your time."

But not for the reasons she believed. Brice would do anything to be in the same room as Alice Whitman. Even if it meant crawling out of bed and coming next door before sunrise. And if it meant helping her mix bread with butter, cinnamon, nutmeg and all those other ingredients, he'd learn to make bread pudding, too.

He'd always had a crush on his best friend's feisty, little redheaded sister, but Adam had threatened to throttle him if he ever came near Alice. At least, that had been the implied threat when they were growing up. Alice had followed them around like a hazel-eyed puppy, though, truth be told, she'd been able to outrun, outsmart and outshine all of the boys on the block. She'd gone on to play soccer and win track medals, too.

She'd sure outrun him after they'd attended her senior prom together on the pretense of him helping her make another boy jealous. She'd asked him, half-joking, when her bouncer of a brother had been too far away to block the idea. He'd accepted, half-serious. If he'd thought it would earn points with her, he would have roughed up the boy who'd hurt her, too. He could still picture her in that emerald-green dress. Could still remember how much he'd wanted to kiss her. If only she'd shown any interest in him at all. But she'd only thanked him for coming to her rescue and had hurried into her house.

That had been nearly a decade ago.

Today was a new day, however, and Alice's big brother was about to be married in an extravagant wedding ceremony, complete with mistletoe, red ribbons and holly. Brice had returned to Atlanta to serve as best man. Because he loved Adam like a brother.

But mostly because he loved Adam's sister in a not-so-brotherly way.

He'd been thrilled to learn that Alice would be one of the bridesmaids. Another chance to be in the same room with her and to stare at her while her brother said his vows. She would be wearing one of those frilly, girlie dresses, too. She might have been a tomboy at heart, but she was all woman in long, flowing dresses.

Now that they were all adults – and he was bigger than Adam – he could finally make his move with Alice. Maybe he should wait until Adam was with his new bride in Hawaii, just to be safe. But then he would move. Not a flirty, fast move. No, he wanted to get to know her all over again in a grown-up way.

Brice wanted to dance with her at the wedding and sit with her in that squeaky swing out on her parents' front porch. He wanted to enjoy the week they'd have together in a slow, let's-fall-in-love kind of way. Walks in the park. Drives around the lake as they took in the Christmas lights. Hot chocolate and old movies. Sitting together in church on Christmas Eve. Opening special presents later as the clock struck midnight.

He'd turned into a sap, but he was enjoying it. Maybe he'd even write a song about Alice and her Amaretto Bread Pudding or Christmas Pudding or whatever kind of pudding she wanted to call it. If only he could convince her that it was time for them to deepen their relationship. Alice could be stubborn when she set her mind to something. Or against something. Time for him to man up and make her see that they needed to cook together all year long.

"What comes after the bread you tormented and tortured?"

She motioned toward the egg carton on the counter. "Now we need to beat several eggs. You crack them into a big bowl and add milk and cream. I like to do half milk and half cream. Then we add the vanilla and the nutmeg and, of course, sugar."

"Okay, milk, cream, eggs. Sounds like the start of a very good omelet to me."

She shook her head. "I can't believe you and I have taken over my mom's kitchen." Then she pointed to the coffee maker. "I could use a refill."

Brice obliged by pouring them both a fresh cup. "Let them sleep while you show me all the things you've learned from Chef What's-His-Name."

"Carrell," she said on a sigh. "You know his name."

"I only watch the show to catch glimpses of you."

She beat the eggs by hand with a definite edge while she frowned at him. "You don't watch the show, so don't even tell me that."

"I do so watch when I can catch it. Seriously, Chef Ready – I mean Chef Remy – is so stuck on himself I'm surprised he can even read a recipe card."

"Hey, he knows all of his recipes by heart."

"Yeah, and all the names in his little black book, too."

"Are you seriously jealous of a chef?"

"I'm not jealous."

But he took the eggshells to the sink and pulverized them with the garbage disposal.

"You have a job you love, so why pick on him?"

Oh, so she thought this was about fame. "I do love what I do. Would you like me to write a jingle for you? Chef Remy, so dreamy. But when I eat his food, I get kind of squeamy."

"You're impossible." She shoved the bowl full of the lemon-colored mixture toward him. "Pour this over the bread, please."

"Yes, ma'am." He did as he was told and then stood back to drink coffee while she chopped pecans. She pulled the bag of coconut out of the refrigerator and frowned at him.

"Remy's a nice man, you know."

"So I hear. Divorced. . . what. . . two. . . three times?"

She glanced sidelong at him. "You're counting that, too?"

"Does he flirt with you?"

"No. Okay, maybe. But he flirts with all the girls."

"And makes them cry."

Ignoring his nursery-rhyme comment, she asked, "Hey, do you want to know about the toppings I'm about to put on this bread pudding?"

Brice moved closer and looked over her shoulder to the mixing bowl. "Yes, I sure do."

"The cherries and coconut meld with the pecans to make the pudding taste like. . . I don't know. . ." She stopped and made a cute face. "But when we add the Amaretto sauce, we take things to a whole new taste dimension."

169

"Christmas," Brice said, reaching for her hand. "This recipe has to taste like Christmas."

She managed to look startled and pleased at the same time. "Yes, that's it. I'm so glad you get that."

"I get that each time I look into your eyes."

Alice lifted her gaze to his. "Chef didn't understand what I was trying to accomplish with this recipe."

"Chef is a blooming idiot."

She giggled and pulled away. "He can be at times, but I'm not supposed to say things like that. I could get fired."

"Or start your own show or. . . come to Memphis and just cook for me."

She turned back. "Brice, are you asking me to be your personal cook?"

Oh, yes. And so much more. "Would you, if I asked?"

Alice just shook her head. "Always joking around."

He guessed that was true. But before this bread pudding was done, he'd be serious with her. Done-and-stick-a-fork-in-it serious.

"Of course, I'm joking." He leaned close, making a first, gentle move. "But if you visited me in Memphis, I'd take you out on the town. We'd dance the two-step and walk along the river and visit Graceland." He stopped, tugged at her long bangs. "And before the night ended, you'd know that I'm a hunka, hunka of burning. . . bread pudding."

Alice stood staring at him, her eyes a burnished gold. "I've never been to Memphis."

Brice held her gaze, savoring the sweetness of vanilla and cinnamon. "We'll have to remedy that, now, won't we?"

She nodded, giving him a tentative smile. "Let's finish this and get it in the oven."

The first of many brush-offs? Oh, no. Brice had many more strategic moves planned. She might love bread pudding, but he knew she also loved big, juicy hamburgers with fries on the side.

"What you doing for dinner?"

"Tonight? Uh, I don't know. Probably something with the

family. Why?"

She wasn't making this easy. "I thought you and I could catch up. Maybe have dinner at the diner."

"That dump is still open?"

"You used to love that dump."

She shoved the pan of her special Christmas concoction into the oven and shut the door. "I still love that dump, and it loves me. Especially my hips."

He loved her hips, too. "They have the best hamburgers in Atlanta."

She closed her eyes. "And those fries. To die for."

He moved close again. "Yep."

She didn't even notice. "Apple pie with ice cream."

Another inch or so. "Uh-huh."

"Remember the nachos? All that taco meat and grated cheese and jalapenos."

"Really spicy."

Alice glanced up and into his eyes. "Brice, maybe I do miss Atlanta after all."

He stood in front of her, his gaze moving over her face. "I miss Atlanta, and I miss you. Don't you think it's time that we get to know each other, Alice?"

She lifted her head, her eyes glistening. "I thought you'd never ask."

Brice cleared the space between them and tugged her close. "That bread pudding smells delicious."

She giggled and smiled. "Christmas bread pudding. It's all about love, after all."

A NOTE FROM LENORA

I love my Christmas Bread Pudding recipe because it is true comfort food. It smells good cooking, and the scents of cinnamon and vanilla make me think of Christmas morning. I remember my mama making biscuit pudding from stale biscuits. This is about the same, but creamier and sweeter. It's delicious fresh out of the oven or leftover and warmed up. It is all about love.

LENORA'S CHRISTMAS BREAD PUDDING (AMARETTO BREAD PUDDING)

Small loaf day-old French/Sourdough bread
3 cups milk
2 cups Half & Half
5 eggs
¼ cup brown sugar
1 cup sugar
1 teaspoon cinnamon
¼ teaspoon nutmeg
1 teaspoon vanilla
Butter for patting bread (as needed)

Topping:
1 cup chopped pecans
1 cup coconut
1 small jar maraschino cherries, drained

Amaretto sauce:
1 ½ cups powdered sugar
½ cup butter
Dollop of Half & Half
¼ cup Amaretto (or 1 tsp. vanilla)

Spray large baking pan with cooking spray. Break up bread in large chunks and place in the baking pan until the entire pan is covered. Pat down. Mix milk, Half & Half, eggs, sugars and spices in large mixing bowl with spoon or mixer on low until eggs are lemony and ingredients are well blended. Pour over bread, making sure to soak completely for five minutes. Sprinkle pecans, cherries and coconut over bread mixture. Bake in 350-degree oven for one hour. (Check every few minutes to make sure the coconut isn't getting too brown. If so, reduce heat to 325 degrees.) Remove from oven and let rest while mixing Amaretto sauce. Melt butter in a pot and whisk in powdered sugar. Stir until smooth and then pour in Half & Half. Add Amaretto and bring to a bubbly boil. Pour sauce over bread pudding while still warm. Serve immediately or reheat as needed. Also good cold.

ABOUT LENORA

LENORA WORTH writes award-winning romance and romantic suspense. Three of her books finaled in the ACFW Carol Awards, and her Love Inspired Suspense, *Body of Evidence*, became a New York Times bestseller. With millions of books in print, Lenora also goes on adventures with her retired husband, Don, and enjoys reading, baking and shopping. . . especially shoe shopping. She enjoys connecting with readers through her web site, www.lenoraworth.com and on Facebook.

SWEET REUNION

BY MISSY TIPPENS

"That was the strangest thing ever," Claire Wilson said to the empty room as she watched her parents drive away. They'd cancelled the dinner reservations they'd made to celebrate her birthday and then had shot out the door with smiles on their faces, claiming a friend needed them. What about their own daughter?

Shaking her head, she closed the front door. An ache at being deserted squeezed her chest. Hadn't she rushed home to Georgia after graduation last week so she'd be here to celebrate her birthday with her parents? Now she wished she had stayed a few extra days on campus with her friends before they all moved on to their jobs and their lives.

"Happy birthday to me," she grumbled as she headed to the sunny yellow kitchen to scrounge up leftovers.

No. She refused to feel sorry for herself. She grabbed her laptop to search for a recipe for something new, something delicious.

A knock sounded at the back door, pulling her away from a

tempting recipe for Chicken Marsala. Lifting the lacy white curtain, she peeked out.

Noah. With a gasp, she mashed her hand against her chest, heart pounding like a herd of charging elephants. What was he doing here?

Everything she'd tried to firmly secure in the past came rushing back at her all at once. Attraction, love . . . rejection, hurt. Mostly the hurt.

She'd managed to avoid close contact with him for the last four years, even though their parents were friends. Not that she'd had to try too hard, as he'd always been conspicuously absent when their two families got together.

And now . . . He looked so handsome. And more mature.

Squashing the pathetic excitement at seeing him on her doorstep, she opened the door.

"Hi." Noah gave a tentative smile.

Was he nervous?

Well, you should be.

"What can I do for you?" She glanced down and noticed the pecan pie in his hands. "Oh." Disappointment killed the hope she'd felt at seeing him again. So he'd only come to bring the annual birthday pie from his mother?

"Happy birthday, Claire." He lifted the pie plate. "I came to deliver this."

"Thank you. Your mom is always sweet to remember me." She reached for the plate.

He pulled it out of her reach. "I would like to bring it in. If that's okay. . ."

Letting her hands drop to her sides, she debated the wisdom of allowing him inside. She had to be careful before putting her heart at risk again.

"Please. I'd like to talk."

His beautiful hazel eyes, so familiar, looked sincere, drawing her in. He'd always had that hold on her. She'd once planned to marry this man. How could she refuse him the chance to talk? Stepping back, she motioned him inside.

"Thanks." He laid the pie on the kitchen counter. "It's been a long time. I've missed you so much."

A burst of anger shot through her so fast it left her dizzy. "Since I haven't heard from you in four years, you have a funny way of showing it. You could have visited me at school or at least have come by when I was home on break."

"I'm sorry. But you have to understand . . ." He reached out for her.

She backed away from his hand. "Don't touch me."

She didn't think she could bear it if he did. She might want to fall into his arms again and beg him to explain why he'd dumped her, destroying her dreams for their future together. Still, she'd deserved an explanation then, and she wanted to hear it now.

With soulful eyes, he held his hands up in surrender. "Please let me try to explain because, as crazy as it sounds, what I did was for you."

Drawing in a deep breath, she straightened her spine, her shoulders rigid. "When you broke up with me, it crushed me. How can you say that was *for* me?" And he'd done it on her birthday, no less. *Four years ago today.*

"You were waffling about going away to college, to your dream university you'd talked about since childhood. I was afraid you'd stay here for me and would resent me later for holding you back."

She turned away. Paced across the kitchen and back. It was true. She had been considering withdrawing from Louisiana State and studying with him at the local college because she hadn't wanted to be five hundred miles away from him. He'd begged her not to miss out, not to give up her top-choice school and scholarship. But she'd insisted that she wanted to stay home. Then he'd suddenly broken up with her, claiming he wanted them to be free to date others in college.

And she'd believed him. "You hadn't fallen out of love with me?"

His gaze softened, and air rushed out of him. "No. I just didn't know any other way to make sure you'd go."

Her heartbeat thrummed. The way he looked at her . . .

"Noah?"

He stepped closer. "I've thought about you every single day for the last four years."

Pushing her hair over her shoulder, Noah brushed his warm fingertips against her neck. "I'm so glad you're back."

She swallowed, nodded. "I took a job here, at the hospital."

"Mom told me you'll be working in radiology. And that you'd moved home this week." A slow smile tilted one side of his mouth. "I had to jump through all kinds of hoops to get her to let me bring over the pie today."

Suddenly, her parents' actions made sense. "And my mom and dad?"

"They're at dinner with my folks. I asked for time to speak to you privately."

Renewed hope took root inside her, yet she tried to hold it at bay. He'd hurt her terribly. She wasn't sure she could trust him again.

He brushed his hand against hers. "I know this may seem sudden to you, and I wouldn't blame you for being angry. But—"

"I have been angry. And I've finally worked through it." Now here he was messing all of that up. She reached inside the cabinet and pulled out two plates. Then she opened a drawer and took out a knife. Anything not to have to stare into his eyes where he might see her hurt . . . and pitiful hope.

As she pushed the knife into the pie, he stilled her hand. "Do you think you can ever forgive me?"

She continued cutting, lifting out two slices and placing them on the plates, stalling. How could she sort out her emotions when they were all over the place? "Honestly, I'm not sure." Hadn't she tried to do just that? To forgive him? Because she'd known she needed to. "I did try. I wanted to forgive you and move on. So I could open up to the other guys I dated."

He winced. "That's only right."

Having been in her parents' kitchen a million times, Noah reached for the coffee maker and started a pot. It felt good

179

having him there. Felt. . . normal. As if all was right in her world once again.

With a snort, she turned away and pulled out two forks. As if one little apology could make things right in her world. No, she couldn't just forgive him in an instant and go back to the way things were.

Was he even asking for that?

As the coffee machine started to hiss, his fingers found hers, and he wrapped her hand in his. "Claire, my feelings are as strong now as they've ever been. I never stopped loving you. I've been praying that you'd understand when I explained why I broke off our relationship."

Her stomach swooped to her knees as she searched his face, taking in the long dark lashes she'd always envied, the familiar scar on his right temple from a bike wreck, the five o'clock shadow that usually hit at about three p.m. She wanted to believe that he hadn't rejected her after all. Had only tried to do what was best. Hadn't she, in the very deepest part of her, been just a tiny bit relieved when she'd felt free to go to her dream school?

"I think I would have resented you if I'd stayed," she admitted.

Sincerity burned in his eyes. "But can you forgive me for hurting you?"

As if her future hung in the balance, she clung to his hand. He looked terrified to hear her answer. Did he truly still care that much?

"Mom said you've had a few casual dates," she said, "but you haven't been serious about anyone. Why's that?"

"Because I've been waiting for you to graduate and return home."

Hope fluttered inside her chest. "And if I hadn't taken a job here?"

"I love being in business with my dad. But I told him I was prepared to move wherever you settled."

"Without knowing how I felt?"

He met her gaze with warmth and sincerity. "I chose to

believe that our love would survive."

"Survive a breakup?"

"Yes."

"And a five-hundred-mile separation?"

"Yes."

"And four years apart?"

He nodded. Took a step closer. Then he brushed his thumb across her cheek. "So, am I right?"

Chill bumps ran along her arms. She thought – *knew* – she still loved him. "Noah, I tried so hard to let you go. I went out with several different guys. Dated one for four months. But I didn't feel a thing beyond friendship."

Taking a deep breath, he relaxed against the counter and pulled her into his arms. "You can't imagine how relieved I am to hear that."

She wrapped her arms around his waist, breathing in the familiar smell of his soap and shampoo. "I never forgot you, either."

He pulled back and looked into her eyes. "But do you still love me?"

Thoughts that had been so jumbled minutes earlier fell into place like the simplest of puzzles. Noah had done the only thing he'd known to do at the time to ensure that she would follow her dreams. And he'd never stopped loving her. Now he was back in her life.

"Yes, I still love you."

A smile stretched across his face, making his eyes dance with joy. "Thank you."

"Thank you for sending me away. And for waiting for me to come home." Words she never would have imagined herself saying.

He touched his forehead to hers. "You've made me the happiest man alive. I feel as if it's *my* birthday." He trailed kisses across her brow, then down along her cheek to her jaw, moving toward—

"Hey," she said, stepping back. "That reminds me. You broke up with me on my birthday four years ago and never gave me the gift you'd been so excited about."

A mischievous smile lit his face. "I still have it."

"Well, maybe it's time you gave it to me."

"We'll see. When the time is right."

"And how will you know the time is right?"

Absently, he rubbed his thumb over her left ring finger. She sucked in her breath and held it. Could it have been. . . ?

Tucking Claire's hand against his chest, Noah pulled her close. He leaned down, his lips near hers. "Soon, I think. Claire, will you go out with me this weekend?"

"It's been four long years," she whispered. "Will you please kiss me?"

"Only if you'll agree to go out with me."

She closed the breath of space between them and touched her lips to his. He froze as if surprised, but quickly recovered, cupping her face in his warm hands and deepening the kiss. She felt as if she'd returned to the place where she truly belonged . . . in his heart and in his arms.

"Is that a yes?" he asked, trying to catch his breath.

"It is. I'd love to go out with you."

"It's a date. A late-birthday celebration."

"What about tonight?"

"Our parents are waiting for us to join them for dinner. And that pie was supposed to be for dessert."

She glanced over at the pie, now with two slices missing. "Oops."

He reared his head back and laughed, a deep belly laugh, just like he'd done when he was a kid. "Let's dump the coffee and wrap up the pie to have it later, after we tell our parents the good news that we're back together."

"Together again thanks to a birthday pie," she said with a smile.

"Yeah. A sweet reunion."

Claire couldn't wait to share the news with their parents. Couldn't wait for the weekend. And for a future that included the love of her life.

A NOTE FROM MISSY

This recipe is special to me because it's one of the first entries I put in the recipe book I received as a wedding shower gift. Shortly after I married, I called my mom from my new home in Georgia to ask for her pecan pie recipe. She dictated it to me by phone from her home in Kentucky. I love to make it for holidays, church luncheons and as an occasional sweet treat.

MOM'S PECAN PIE

1 cup pecans, chopped
3 large eggs
1 cup sugar
1 cup white corn syrup
½ stick melted butter
1 teaspoon vanilla
One pie crust (I use a store-bought rolled, refrigerated crust)

Since this is a high-sugar pie, dust a little flour on both sides of the crust. Place in pie plate and crimp edges. Cover the bottom of crust with the chopped pecans. Mix all other ingredients together and pour over pecans. (This is my mom's trick for making the pecans yummy, sweet and crispy. It coats them with the pie filling, and they float to the top.) Bake at 350 degrees for 45 to 50 minutes. Shake a little, and it should be mostly jelled. Remove and let cool. Enjoy!

ABOUT MISSY

After more than twelve years pursuing a career in writing, **MISSY TIPPENS**, a pastor's wife and mom of three from near Atlanta, Georgia, made her first sale to Harlequin Love Inspired in 2007. Her books have since been nominated for the Booksellers Best, ACFW Carol Award, Gayle Wilson Award of Excellence, Maggie Award, Beacon Contest, RT Reviewer's Choice Award and Romance Writers of America's RITA. Visit Missy at www.missytippens.com.

GINGERBREAD LADIES

BY JANET TRONSTAD

Miles City, Montana Territory, 1887

Railroad smoke mingled with the damp outside air, but that wasn't the main reason Anya Cleary wrapped her hands in the folds of her shawl as she stood on the train platform in the frontier town of Miles City. The patches on her worn gray dress might label her as poor, but her chapped hands confirmed it. And she was suddenly feeling uncertain of her welcome.

She'd spent the train ride here from New York sitting across the aisle from Marabelle Huntington, the other mail-order bride, who had chanced to ride west with her. Marabelle's traveling bag was overflowing with lace and silk garments. Anya wasn't usually given to envy, but last night as the train rolled into the Montana Territory, a worry had started to gnaw at her. What if her intended husband, Howard Smith, was disappointed in the bride he was receiving?

Middle-aged and plain, Anya had been relieved that Howard hadn't asked if she was pretty. But now she feared he

186

might have forgotten to ask. They'd only had time to write a few letters, and he'd seemed mostly concerned with providing a mother for his daughter. But that didn't mean he wouldn't also have the same expectations as other men.

Of course, it was much too late to fret, she told herself firmly, as she looked around the platform. For better or for worse, this would be her new life. She didn't see anyone around who fit her intended's description. A blacksmith, Howard had said he was over six feet tall and had dark hair. She would know him because he would have his precious daughter, Elizabeth, with him, he'd said.

Just then Anya heard an excited squeal. She saw a young girl in a pink ruffled dress running toward Marabelle. A prosperous-looking older man followed after the child and caught the girl just as Marabelle drew back from the child. Anya knew the other woman was careful not to wrinkle her silk dresses, and small arms could do just that.

She forced herself to look away from Marabelle's new family and search the platform for her own.

Finally, she heard a call.

"Miss Cleary."

Anya turned and saw a man and girl walking toward her. This girl had none of the exuberance of the one in the pink dress and walked with her head down.

The man reached Anya first. "I'm pleased to meet you, Ma'am."

Her heart sank. She'd never expected him to be handsome like this. Or to be wearing a gray suit that looked new. She was sure to disappoint him.

"Say hello to your new mother, Elizabeth," Howard said, still looking at Anya.

His smile was so steady that Anya began to hope he didn't notice her lack of polish.

"She's not my mother," the young girl whispered. "My mother is much prettier."

Anya's face heated.

"Apologize right now, young lady," Howard demanded.

Elizabeth looked up, finally, and Anya's heart broke at the misery on the child's small face.

"I'm sorry," the girl said, although she clearly didn't mean it.

"You should be happy she got here in time for the mother/daughter Christmas tea at school," Howard added, his voice softening. Then his eyes twinkled. "She'll look a lot better sitting beside you with a tea cup in her hand than I would."

Anya knew he was trying to smooth things over, but Elizabeth didn't look convinced.

Then the girl in pink walked over.

"My new mother has a parasol to wear to the tea," she bragged to Elizabeth. "And she's going to bring crushed lemon drops. She said all the fancy ladies in New York stir the candies into their hot tea and let the pieces melt."

With that, the girl ran off to catch up with her father and Marabelle.

Howard grunted. "I don't know what the teacher was thinking, having a tea like that."

"I expect she was just hoping to give the girls some holiday cheer," Anya murmured, her heart sinking. Her trunk was small and didn't contain a dress any more fashionable than the one she wore. She'd never had anything like a parasol. She had no jewels or stylish hair combs. She didn't even have any candy except a small bag of peppermints that she'd bought for Elizabeth's Christmas stocking.

"We have to bring something for the tea," Elizabeth said, not looking at her father or at Anya. "Everyone does."

"We'll buy some soda crackers at the store," Howard said. "The tea is tomorrow, and Miss Cleary will want to rest tonight."

"I could . . . " Anya began to say, although she had no idea what she could do to make things better for Elizabeth.

Howard turned to her. "The reverend's out of town until Christmas, so we'll need to wait a couple of days to get married. I'll spend the nights in my blacksmith shop and leave the house to you and Elizabeth until then."

Anya nodded.

"Take Miss Cleary to the wagon," Howard told his daughter. "I'll get her trunk."

Elizabeth nodded and started toward the edge of the railroad platform.

"We'll stop at the store," Howard added for Anya. "If you need anything, let me know."

She wondered if that was a hint that she needed a better dress. She shook her head though. It was enough that he'd paid for her train fare. She didn't want to press him.

Anya had to hurry to catch up to Elizabeth.

When they stopped at the mercantile, Howard bought a few pounds of soda crackers while Anya looked at everything else. The store smelled of cinnamon and tea. Glass jars of penny candies sat on the long counter.

"We might want to get some supplies for cooking," Howard said as he walked over to her. "We've been taking most of our meals at the boarding house across the street from us. But, I was hoping that now that you're here . . ."

"I can cook," Anya assured him, glad to be able to show she would be useful. She glanced at Elizabeth. The girl was standing across the room at a counter of ribbons and fabrics. Unfortunately, Anya had never learned to do fine sewing. What fabric she had was always cut down from another garment, usually one that had come from the church poor box. Until her grandmother died a few months ago, all of the money she'd earned as a scrub woman had gone for food and lodging for the two of them.

Howard seemed pleased that she could cook though.

"Give us bags of flour and sugar," he called out to the store clerk. "And . . .?" Howard looked to Anya with a question in his eyes. "We're out of everything."

"Add some vanilla and cinnamon," Anya said as she her gaze roamed over the shelves. "Baking soda and molasses. Salt and some butter, if you have it. Maybe a large ham." She looked over at Howard, and he nodded.

"Dried apples and raisins would be good, too," Anya added. "Some eggs and a tin of ginger. Lard, of course."

By the time she was finished ordering supplies, the stack on the counter was substantial.

"It's too much," she said as she turned to Howard. "We can do without some of that."

"Not at Christmas." Howard told the clerk to add the items to his bill. "And give me a couple dozen of those ribbons over there." He nodded toward where Elizabeth stood. "Some red and green ones and . . ." He looked at Anya. "How about blue for you? To match your eyes."

"I don't need—" Anya began.

He cut her off. "It's a present for Christmas. Give us some yellow and white ones, too."

After the wagon was loaded, Howard helped Anya climb up to the seat. Then he reached for Elizabeth, but the girl said she'd rather sit in back with the supplies.

Anya's face heated once more. The child wasn't going to accept her easily, and Anya was well aware that Howard was marrying her more to have a mother for Elizabeth than a wife for him. What if she couldn't be the mother he needed her to be? She usually got along well with children, but she wasn't sure Elizabeth would ever soften toward her.

It only took a few minutes to drive to Howard's house. The small building, made of raw wood, had a wide porch and two glass windows in front. Anya could smell a pot of beans and bacon cooking when he opened the door.

"We'll eat and get settled in," he said as he led her into the house.

Anya was tired, and it was dusk by the time they finished eating. Elizabeth had already divided the stack of ribbons, taking most of them for herself and leaving a dark-blue one, three yellow ones, and four white ones for Anya.

The house had two bedrooms, and Howard led Anya to his room.

"I'll join you here in a few days," he whispered as he opened the door. "I want the church's blessing on us first though."

"Me, too," Anya agreed softly, grateful he felt the same way.

Sleep claimed her soon after she changed into her nightclothes and stretched out on the comfortable bed. It was completely dark outside when a noise woke her. She listened for a minute, and then she heard it again. Someone was crying.

Anya lit the candle by her bed and walked out into the main part of the house. Elizabeth's door was open and, when she heard the sob again, she knew it was coming from the girl.

"Elizabeth," she whispered as she stood in the doorway.

In the night shadows, Anya could see the girl stiffen under her covers. The child kept her back to the door though, no doubt hoping she looked like she was sleeping.

"Can I help?" Anya asked after a moment.

There was no answer, not that she had expected one. Slowly, she backed away. Elizabeth was clearly unhappy, and Anya could hardly blame her. The poor thing had lost her mother not that long ago and was now being expected to accept another woman in her place.

In the kitchen, she sat down at the table, planning to get herself a glass of water before going back to bed. But then her gaze drifted over the supplies stacked on the counter. The bag of crackers lay on top of the flour sack, and she remembered the girl in pink taunting Elizabeth with her good fortune in having Marabelle for a new mother.

Anya knew how unkind children could be, and she vowed then and there to do her best by Elizabeth. The Christmas tea, she told herself, was the place to start. She could give Elizabeth something much better than crackers to pass around.

Standing up, she walked over to the hook that held an old apron. She remembered one of her grandmother's recipes.

An hour later, as the smell of gingerbread cookies spread throughout the house, Anya looked up and saw Elizabeth standing in the doorway of the kitchen.

"What are you doing?" the girl asked, her face still puffy from her tears.

"Making gingerbread ladies for your tea," she answered.

A floured knife sat on the counter beside the cookies. Anya had cut the gingerbread cookies into the shape of waltzing ladies, each cookie a woman with a swirling skirt and a high twist of hair. The girl approached the counter, and Anya held her breath.

"They're not decorated yet," she told her. "I plan to make a sugar icing and sprinkle them with crumbs of peppermint candy. Then I'll tie ribbons around their neck like jewelry."

Anya had already taken her yellow and white ribbons and cut them into tiny strips for the necks of her ladies.

"They'll be beautiful," Elizabeth said softly. "How'd you make them dance like that?"

"My grandmother used to make me ladies like this when I was your age," Anya said and smiled. "I used to help with the decorating, and you can, too, if you'd like."

Elizabeth nodded. "We can use some of my red ribbons, too. For Christmas."

They worked together making the gingerbread ladies look elegant and festive.

The next afternoon, Howard drove all three of them to the schoolhouse. Regular classes had been closed for the holiday, and pine branches were placed around the edges of the room. Four large tables were arranged with brown teapots centered on them. A dozen other girls and their mothers were already there.

Anya and Howard stood in the doorway as Elizabeth carefully carried a tray of gingerbread ladies into the room.

The gasps of delight from the girls at the tables made Anya glow, but nothing warmed her heart as much as hearing Elizabeth proudly say, "My new mother made them. Her grandmother used to make them for her, and now she's making them for me."

"Thank you," Howard said as he reached over and took Anya's hand. "You're just the one we need to make our family complete."

A NOTE FROM JANET

My family made many different kinds of Christmas cookies while I was growing up, but my all-time favorite has always been the cut-out cookies, either traditional sugar cookies or gingerbread ones, shaped like stars, trees or men. Even today, at some time during the holiday season, I will sit down for an afternoon of reading Christmas stories with a plate of those cookies at my side. This recipe is, to the best of my recollection, the one my mother used when making gingerbread cookies.

GINGERBREAD CHRISTMAS COOKIES

1 cup sugar
1 cup molasses
¾ cup oil *
½ cup hot water
2 eggs
1 teaspoon baking soda
½ teaspoon salt
2 teaspoons cinnamon
2 teaspoons ginger
6 to 7 cups white flour

Combine sugar, molasses, oil and water in large bowl. Add eggs. Mix dry ingredients together and add to wet ingredients. Mix well. Cover and refrigerate overnight. Roll dough out on a lightly-floured surface. Cut into desired shapes. Bake at 350 degrees for 10 minutes. Yield 4 dozen cookies, depending on shapes cut. These cookies freeze well and are softer and more flavorful after freezing.
　*Used to be ¾ cup lard

ABOUT JANET

JANET TRONSTAD is the USA Today and Publisher's Weekly best-selling author of the long-standing Dry Creek series for Harlequin Love Inspired. Born on a Montana farm, Janet is noted for the warmth of her fictitious town, set near her father's birthplace in southeastern Montana. Her books have been translated into many languages, including French, Italian, German, and Dutch, and over three million copies are in print. Find Janet on Facebook.

A SWEET REMEDY

BY WINNIE GRIGGS

Eunice paused as Dusty stopped to sniff something under one of the shrubs that marked her backyard's boundary. Experience had taught her not to look too closely at the object of these canine investigations.

She gave Dusty's leash a tug. "Come on, pooch, time to move on."

Eunice wasn't big on pets, which was why she didn't have any of her own. But her sister, Anna, had conned her into dog sitting this weekend in exchange for the use of that killer-red designer dress she'd bought recently, said use to occur at a future event of Eunice's choosing.

"Right now," she said, raising a brow Dusty's way, "I'm not so sure which of us got the better end of that deal."

Except that it had provided her with *one* unexpected benefit. Mark Connors, her new neighbor, was out on his back patio, typing away on a laptop. He'd moved into the house next door three weeks ago, and she'd been intrigued by him from the moment she'd seen him in his driveway and had exchanged hellos. She wasn't exactly sure why she found him so interesting, except that he had kind eyes.

When she'd said as much to Anna, her sister had told her that was a ridiculously romantic notion. But what was wrong with romantic notions?

With Mark's profile to her now and his attention focused elsewhere, Eunice was free to study him at will. The door behind him opened, and a young boy, who looked about nine years old, came out. Mark had a kid? A joint-custody situation perhaps? The boy talked to Mark for a few minutes, then headed her way.

"Hi." He waved toward Dusty. "What kind of dog is he?"

Eunice smiled at the boy. "Dusty's a collie-poodle mix." She held out a hand. "I'm Eunice Perkins. And you are . . .?"

He gave her hand a firm shake, his gaze never leaving the dog. "I'm Kevin. Can I pet him?"

"Of course."

While the boy stooped to ruffle Dusty's fur, Eunice sneaked another glance at her neighbor. To her surprise, Mark glanced up from his keyboard and smiled her way. It was much warmer than the polite smiles he'd given her when they'd happened to spot each other across their respective yards. She tucked her hair behind her ear as she smiled back. A moment later he returned to his work.

Oh well, it was a start.

"Ow!"

Eunice turned back to the boy, lingering thoughts of her neighbor evaporating. "What is it? Did Dusty do something to you?"

"No, a bee stung my hand." Kevin sounded as if he was in pain but was trying not to let it show. His grimace, though, gave him away.

"Here, let me have a look at that." She took the boy's hand, studying the red welt that was forming. "You're not allergic, are you?"

"I don't think so."

"Kevin, are you okay?" Mark started across the yard.

"He's got a bee sting," Eunice replied for the boy. She gently scraped a fingernail over the welt, removing the stinger embedded in the skin.

Mark closed the distance between them quickly, a concerned look on his face. If she were guessing, she'd say he didn't know how to handle a bee sting.

"I have just the thing to take care of it." She nodded toward her house. "Why don't you let me doctor it for you?"

Mark rubbed the back of his neck. "If it's not a bother . . ."

She smiled to ease his worry. "No bother at all. Just follow me."

What kind of shape had she left her house in? The bedroom was a shambles, but she was pretty sure she'd closed the door to keep Dusty out. And although lunch dishes still sat in the sink, at least she'd cleaned the table.

"I really appreciate your help," Mark said, walking beside her. "I'm not used to dealing with kid-type emergencies."

"So Kevin isn't a regular at your place?" Was she being subtle enough with her probing?

"Oh. Kevin's not mine. He's my sister's kid. He's staying with me this week."

"Mom and Dad are on a cruise," Kevin added. Then he grimaced. "They're calling it a second honeymoon."

Mark ruffled the boy's hair good-naturedly. "Give 'em a break, Kev. This is their first vacation with just the two of them since before you came along."

Kevin nodded with a sheepish smile. "I know. But did they have to call it that?"

Eunice hid a grin as she opened the door that led from the back porch to kitchen. "Have a seat." She waved toward the breakfast bar. "I just need to grab a few things."

Kevin hopped on a stool, but Mark remained standing. "Eunice, is it?"

She grimaced. "Yes."

He tilted his head to the side. "Don't you like your name?"

She opened the pantry, hiding her face from him. "It's so old-fashioned and just, well, spinsterish. There isn't even a good nickname to take from it."

He laughed, and she liked the warm, rich sound of it.

"That's not how I see it," he said. "There's a certain charm to it. And in this day and age, it's unique, which means you can make it your own."

"I guess I'll have to," she said with a chuckle.

Was he just being kind? Regardless, his words raised her spirits.

He moved closer. "Is there something I can help you with?"

Both liking and feeling unnerved by his nearness, she pointed to her right. "While I'm mixing up the paste, you can grab a cloth from that drawer and clean the area around the sting."

He moved to do as she asked without questioning her instructions. That was nice, too.

When she'd mixed the paste to a consistency she was happy with, she turned back to her visitors and faced the boy across the counter. "Let's see if this will take care of that sting."

"What is it?" Mark asked.

"A home remedy made with baking soda and water. It'll neutralize the acid in the bee venom."

He raised a skeptical brow, but he didn't discourage her from trying it. She slathered a thick coat of the paste on the raised welt, then straightened and smiled at Kevin. "There. That should start feeling better pretty quick."

Kevin nodded. "It feels better already."

Eunice hid her skepticism and pointed a warning finger at him. "You need to keep that on for at least fifteen minutes." She moved to the sink to rinse her hands and tried to adopt a casual tone. "If you're not in a hurry, you two can wait here, so I can check it out when you rinse it off."

"We're in no hurry," Mark answered.

Was she imagining the interest in his tone?

"You're good at that," Mark indicated Kevin's hand. "Is it because you're around kids a lot? Or are you just good with bee stings?"

"A little of both. I'm a nurse in a pediatrician's office."

"Then we're lucky to have you next door."

Not quite sure how to respond, Eunice searched for a change of subject and spotted the plastic container on the counter. "How do you gentlemen feel about peanut butter fudge?"

Kevin's eyes lit up. "I like it, a *lot*."

"Me, too," Mark chimed.

"Then you must do me the favor of helping eat this up." She grabbed the container and lifted the lid. "I made it yesterday because I had a sudden craving. Unfortunately, I don't know how to make a small batch, and I can't possibly eat it all."

She'd planned to carry the leftovers to the office on Monday, but this seemed like a much better use of the candy. Kevin and Mark each selected a piece of the sweet treat.

Kevin took one bite and then closed his eyes in a pose of exaggerated bliss. "Oh man, this is the *best*!"

Mark smiled. "I have to agree. Best peanut butter fudge I've ever tasted."

"Well, thank you, gentlemen. It's an old family recipe." And one of her favorite comfort foods.

Dusty approached, his tail wagging hopefully.

"Sorry buddy," she said, "you'll have to settle for a dog biscuit."

"Is the dog new?" Mark asked as she fetched the biscuit. "I haven't seen him around here before."

Just the thought the he'd been paying attention made her feel tingly inside. "He's not *mine*, either. I'm just dog sitting while my sister and her family are on vacation."

"Like Uncle Mark is doing for me." Kevin reached for another piece of fudge.

Mark smiled. "Not *quite* the same."

"You know what I mean." Then Kevin's eyes widened as he spied something in her living room. "Hey, Uncle Mark, look at those baseballs."

He glanced where his nephew was pointing, then back at

Eunice. "You're a baseball fan?"

"Dyed in the wool." She waved toward her living room. "Look closer if you like."

They took her up on her offer, and both guys crossed into the living room and studied the display with interest.

"Impressive," Mark said. "Where did you get these?"

"My dad took me to ballgames when I was younger. I have fond memories of the two of us sitting in the stands, cheering on our favorite teams." She pointed to the baseball on the end of the row. "This one," she moved her finger to the next one, "and this one are two I caught myself. And the one next to them is one my dad caught."

She gestured to the whole collection. "The rest we collected by waiting after the games to get signatures on them from our favorite players."

"What about your sister?" Mark asked.

"She was more into fashion and dance class. A real girly girl." Eunice had always envied Anna's graceful and effortless femininity.

Mark studied her with warm approval. "I've always found tomboys more interesting myself."

Her cheeks heated under his gaze. Goodness, she was blushing like a teenager.

Eunice quickly turned to Kevin. "I think we can rinse your hand now." She led him to the kitchen, very much aware of Mark following behind. As she turned on the faucet, she risked a glance over her shoulder and caught Mark watching her.

He grinned and snagged another piece of the fudge. "Hope you don't mind. This stuff is addictive."

"Not at all. Help yourself."

She helped Kevin rinse his hand. "How does it feel?"

"A lot better. Thanks."

She handed him a towel, then turned to Mark. "It'll probably start to itch as it heals. Some hydrocortisone cream will help with that."

Mark nodded. "We're heading to the grocery store this afternoon. I'll pick some up." He clapped Kevin on the back.

"We've taken up enough of Eunice's time. What say we let her get on with whatever she'd planned to do today?"

Then he smiled at Eunice. "Thanks again. Kev was definitely better off in your hands than mine."

"It was my pleasure." She reached for the container of fudge. "Why don't y'all take a few pieces with you?"

Kevin didn't wait to be told twice. "Yes ma'am," he said as he retrieved two pieces.

Mark rolled his eyes. "Please blame my sister for his manners. Not me."

She laughed, liking the way Mark seemed so at ease with her. "A growing boy needs to eat. And peanut butter is packed with protein."

Kevin struck a virtuous pose. "See, Uncle Mark, it's *good* for me."

Mark cuffed his nephew playfully on the shoulder. "Yeah, *that's* why you eat it." Then he turned back to Eunice. "We'll get out of your way now. Come on, Kev."

Eunice led them to the door, then watched them walk away. As she shut the door, she looked down at Dusty, feeling oddly empty.

"So what do you think? That could be the start of something wonderful. Or it could be nothing more than a pleasant encounter. We'll just have to wait and see. The next move is his."

After petting Dusty's head, she reached for a piece of fudge. Before she'd taken her first bite, however, there was a rap on the door. Had they forgotten something? Eunice quickly crossed the room and opened the door.

There stood Mark. He was smiling, but she thought she detected a note of uncertainty behind his expression.

"Did you forget something?"

"It occurred to me that a mere thank you isn't enough."

"Oh, there's no need—"

He held up a hand. "Yes, there is. And I know just the thing. How about I take you to Mitchell University's baseball game next Saturday?"

She shook her head. "Thanks. But that's the rivalry game with State. Those tickets have been sold out for weeks."

His expression took on a self-assured edge. "I can get tickets. The coach is a buddy of mine."

"Then you're on." She thought again about his warm, kind eyes, deciding that his smile was a good match for them.

And this time there was no empty feeling when he left.

Because now she knew it was *definitely* the start of something wonderful.

A NOTE FROM WINNIE

This recipe is one of the first things my mom taught me to cook. I remember her standing over me and my younger sister as we made batches of this sweet treat. Sometimes it didn't turn out just right, and we had to eat it with a spoon. I actually enjoyed eating it this way. I'll even confess to deliberately sabotaging it on a few occasions so that it wouldn't harden properly. I hope you'll enjoy this fudge as much as my family and I do.

PEANUT BUTTER FUDGE

3 cups sugar
½ teaspoon salt
1 ½ cups milk
1 1/2 cups peanut butter (creamy or chunky)
¼ cup butter
1 teaspoon vanilla

In heavy 4-quart saucepan, combine sugar and salt. Stir in milk. Over medium heat, stir constantly until mixture reaches bubbly boil. Continue boiling without stirring until mixture reaches soft ball stage or 234 degrees. Quickly stir in peanut butter until well mixed. Remove from heat and add butter and vanilla. Do not stir. Cool to 110 degrees. Beat until fudge thickens and shine fades. Quickly spread in a buttered 8-inch or 9-inch pan. Cool completely. Cut into squares.

ABOUT WINNIE

WINNIE GRIGGS is a multi-published, award-winning author of Historical (and occasionally Contemporary) romances that focus on "Small Towns, Big Hearts, Amazing Grace." She is also a list maker and a lover of dragonflies and holds an advanced degree in the art of procrastination. Winnie loves to hear from readers. Learn about her new releases and stay in touch through her web site, www.winniegriggs.com, Facebook or email winnie@winniegriggs.com.

BAKING MEMORIES

BY DANA CORBIT

"They're a little skinny, don't you think?"

Shelly McCall leaned in to examine the cut sugar cookies that Troy Wilder was transferring to her mother's best baking sheet. They looked more like Flat Stanley figures than the thick-cut Christmas angels, bells and trees she'd planned to serve later for her family's Christmas Eve celebration.

No matter how amazing her boyfriend was, what had she been thinking, letting him help her bake *these cookies*? Especially not when her relatives would be showing up from all over southern Indiana in three hours. Why was she piling more strain on a holiday season that had already stressed her out to the top of the Blue Spruce lighting the living room and to the toe of her stocking hanging on the mantel? Christmas just wasn't the same without Nana. Too much shopping. Too many crowds. Never enough time. And if these cookies didn't turn out, she would be under the gun to make another batch. So far, they just weren't good enough.

"What now?" Troy stared down at the tray, his wavy brown

hair falling forward over his wire-frame glasses. He set his rolling pin aside and brushed his hands off on his jeans, leaving twin flour handprints on his thighs. "Am I measuring the flour wrong? Or forgetting the lemon juice for the sour milk? Or adding too much flour to the dough?"

Though Troy's grin never wavered, Shelly didn't miss the slight annoyance in his tone. Maybe she deserved that. She'd been more critical than she'd planned during their baking session, but he should have understood that these cookies needed to be perfect. They had to be.

She dotted his nose with flour and then turned to wash her hands in the sink. "Relax. I just meant that you're rolling the dough too thin. The cookies will get too brown when they bake. They'll be crispy instead of chewy."

He reached over and tugged on her long ponytail. "Oh, no. We couldn't have that."

Ignoring his sarcasm and the spray of flour he'd probably left in her dark hair, she demonstrated again how to roll the dough to the proper one-eighth-inch thickness. "And, besides, Nana's sugar cookies were always really fat."

"Well, why didn't you say so?"

"I just did."

Troy wadded the dough into a ball and rolled it out just as she'd demonstrated, but instead of cutting a cookie, he ripped off a piece of dough and tossed it into his mouth.

"Quit eating that!"

He shrugged. "Thankless work. Just finding some benefits."

Her jaw tightened. "I already thanked you for helping."

"I wouldn't turn down a kiss of gratitude to go with it." He winked at her automatic frown.

Where his flirting usually would have set a swarm of butterflies free to flutter in her tummy, now only a lump of resentment formed there. What was wrong with him? Why couldn't he understand how important this was to her?

"Come on. I told you this is the first time I've ever made my grandmother's special recipe. You promised to take it seriously."

He nodded, his head lowered. "I know. I promised."

"Even though we lost Nana, if we make her cookies for Christmas Eve, and we get them right, it will be like . . . she's still with us."

She hated that her voice quavered, but it frustrated her even more that Troy noticed, too. He watched her for several long seconds, and then his lips lifted again.

"If you wanted to get them right, you should have thought about that before asking for *my* help."

"Maybe I should have," she quipped.

He was only trying to cheer her up, to make her smile the way he always did, and yet everything he said and did this afternoon aggravated her. They'd been balancing atop an egg carton all day, and it was only a matter of time until some of the shells cracked. He gave a scowl that no one would take seriously, performed an elaborate stretch and returned to work.

"How's this one?" He pointed to a gingerbread man that was as nice as a cookie she might have cut herself.

"Now that's what we're talking about."

She couldn't help smiling as she watched him work, so focused on the Santa's sleigh he lifted off the counter. This was Troy, the man who'd tunneled his way into her heart nearly a year before and had staked his claim. Why was she being so nasty to him? What was wrong with *her*?

His tray filled, Troy washed and dried his hands and then stepped behind her. At the first touch of his fingers on her surprisingly tight shoulders, she let her head fall forward with a sigh. This had to have been the longest day ever.

"The holidays are going to be tough for you this year." He paused, rubbing deep circles on her neck. "Didn't your grandmother pass away around this time last year. A year ago—"

"Today," she somehow managed.

Troy turned her to face him and then took her hands. "Tell me more about Nana."

A rush of memories filled her thoughts in pastel colors and soothing sounds. She could almost smell the sweet aromas that used to waft from Nana's kitchen and could taste the love baked into all of those treats.

"She was smart and funny and sweet. The type of person who made everyone else feel at home. Whose smile lit up the room like a crystal chandelier."

"You do realize you just described yourself, don't you?"

He traced his fingertips over her palms, leaving a trail of tingles on her skin. Shelly pulled her hands away and dropped them to her sides.

"No one will ever be like Nana. She was one-of-a-kind."

"And she has a wonderful granddaughter."

She shrugged. "I just wish you'd had the chance to meet her. But she was too sick the last time we tried to visit. You would have loved her."

"If she was anything like you, I know I would have." He brushed his lips over hers, but just as her eyelids fluttered closed, he pulled back. "If we hope to have her special cookies ready for your mom's dinner tonight, we'd better get to work."

Shelly blinked but pushed back her disappointment, grabbing the rolling pin and another lump of dough. "Then move out of the way, and I'll show you how it's done."

Within minutes, two more cookie sheets were covered with Santas, angels and reindeer. She slid two of the pans into the oven, her spirits rising as quickly as the cookies did.

"What do you think?" She indicated the baking treats.

"I think we have some down time before our next cookie duties." He pulled her into his arms, her hip resting against the oven door handle.

"We could start cleaning this mess," she began, but as he nipped at her neck, the dirty measuring cups and sticky beaters on the counter seemed to melt away. Though the brush of his breath over her skin raised delicious goose bumps on her arms, when he pressed his lips to hers, sinking into the sweetness they always shared, she relaxed for the first time in days. Her heart was his alone.

With closed eyes, she breathed in the shower-fresh scent of him. So familiar. So warm. So . . . pungent. Her eyes popped open to the acrid scent. Slowly, they turned back to the oven.

"No!"

She pushed him aside and jerked open the oven door. Grabbing oven mitts, she withdrew two sheets of burned cookies and set them on the stovetop. She shook her head. How could this have happened? Okay, she'd forgotten to set the oven timer, but there was no way that much time could have passed. They'd only been kissing for a few seconds. Or was it minutes? She wanted to believe she hadn't let the time slip away while lost in Troy's warm brown eyes, and yet the little charred lumps on the cookie sheet suggested otherwise.

"I've ruined everything. I only wanted to do this one thing for Nana, and I can't even get that right."

Shelly turned to the stove so Troy wouldn't see her disappointment. They were only cookies after all. He would never understand. But as she stared down at those trays of burned cookies, she couldn't hold back the tears. To her humiliation, her shoulders shook.

Troy gently turned her to face him, searching her eyes for answers she couldn't give. How could she explain to him what she didn't understand herself? She could only let him fold her in his arms, her tears dampening his shirt.

"Honey, it's only one batch," he said as he pulled back from her. "We can make more. Nana probably burned a batch or two from this recipe over the years."

She swallowed, her throat hot. "No, she didn't."

"You can't know that. You couldn't have been around every—"

"It . . . isn't . . . even . . . hers."

He shook his head. "You're not making sense. What isn't hers?"

It seemed so silly now. So awful and deceitful. He deserved an explanation though, so she took a deep breath and let out the words as she exhaled. "The recipe."

"The what? Wait." He stopped, stared, as understanding dawned. "You mean to tell me we've had all this drama over Nana's special sugar cookies, and the recipe isn't hers?"

She nodded, her shoulders curling inward.

"So why the . . . story?"

"Go ahead and say it. The lie." She brushed at the tears covering her cheeks. "You don't know how much I wanted this recipe to be Nana's. We'd always planned to write hers down, including a pinch of this and a smidgen of that. But then she died, and . . ."

"It died with her," he said, finishing the sentence.

"I kept experimenting with other recipes, trying to make cookies as amazing as Nana's, but I couldn't get it right." Looking up from her hands, she caught him watching her again. "This must seem so silly to you. All this for a recipe."

He put his thumb under her chin and lifted it. "No, honey. It isn't silly because it isn't about a recipe at all. Or even about something you've lost. It's about losing *someone* who was very special to you."

Troy's face blurred as tears pooled in her eyes once more. His thumb brushed away the first to trail down her cheek.

"So tell me," he began, smiling again, "whose cookies have we just nuked?"

Because he wouldn't want her to notice, Shelly pretended she didn't see that his eyes were damp now was well. "I tried Amie's grandma's recipe a few weeks ago, and those cookies were as close as any I'd tasted to Nana's. So I claimed them as hers. I didn't want to let her Christmas Eve tradition die, too."

Troy ruffled her hair. "The cookies won't keep your grandmother with you on Christmas Eve and always. Your memories will do that. She's probably looking down from Heaven at you right now, tickled that you wanted to keep her tradition alive. Especially that you went to such lengths to do it."

He took her hand and led her back to the counter where they'd left the mixing bowl and rolling pin. "We have more cookies to make."

"You're not going to tell my family about this, are you?"

"Oh, no. Not me. But one day you'll want to tell the whole story. It will be great for laughs."

She shook her head. She didn't feel like laughing now, and it would be a long time before she would see this story as anything but painful. Her thoughts still clinging to the past, to memories threatening to slip through her fingers faster than the water she used to rinse the rubber spatula, she startled at the sound of Troy clearing his throat.

"When you do tell your story, Shelly, I want to be there to hear it."

She shook her head, her pulse pounding in her ears. "What are you saying?"

"That it's about time for us to start some holiday traditions of our own. Like gifts of jewelry on Christmas Eve."

She could only stare as he grabbed his coat off the kitchen chair and pulled a velvet box from the pocket. He popped it open to reveal a sparkling solitaire engagement ring nestled inside.

"Any thoughts?" He pressed his lips together, waiting.

Without hesitation, Shelly threw her arms around his neck and kissed him, sealing their promise without a need for words. They held each other, sharing their dreams for a life together, before she finally pulled back from him.

"Yes, jewelry is a good tradition," she said, pausing to kiss the forehead of the man she adored. "That and making stolen cookies."

A NOTE FROM DANA

This recipe and story are both dear to me as Shelly's story is similar to my own. My great-grandmother, Myrtle Bowley, made the most wonderful sugar cookies, and when she passed away, we lost her recipe along with her. When I tried my friend's aunt's recipe, and it was similar to Grandma's, I claimed it as my own. I never tried to pass the recipe off as Grandma Bowley's, but I might have considered it. Using my extensive cookie-cutter collection, I make these cookies for Christmas and other holidays, always frosting them with butter cream icing.

STOLEN SOFT SUGAR COOKIES

5 cups flour
2 cups sugar
2 teaspoons baking powder
2 unbeaten eggs
½ teaspoon salt
1 teaspoon vanilla
¾ teaspoon baking soda
1 cup shortening
¾ cup sour milk (add 1 teaspoon lemon juice)

Sift flour. Cream shortening and sugar. Add eggs one at a time. Add vanilla. Add baking powder, salt and baking soda. Add sour milk, alternating with flour. Chill two hours. Roll out dough 1/8 inch thick. Cut shapes and place on cookie sheet sprayed with nonstick spray. Bake at 400 degrees for 9 minutes. Cool a few minutes on the pan before moving to aluminum foil to cool completely. Frost.

ABOUT DANA

Features editor-turned-fiction writer **DANA CORBIT** is the award-winning author of sixteen novels for Harlequin Love Inspired and Guideposts Books. Her popular works have included the *Hickory Ridge* miniseries and the *Wedding Bell Blessings* trilogy. Always an Indiana girl at heart, Corbit lives in southeast Michigan with her husband, three nearly-grown daughters and two tubby kitties. Find her books on www.harlequin.com, friend her on Facebook, or follow her on Twitter.

AN IRISH BLESSING

BY DEB KASTNER

"Why, Em! Another single Irish rose? That makes how many now, my dear?" Jo Murphy, the elderly redhead, hooted with glee and bobbed her head, sending her wild curls bouncing. "Not to mention that they've been delivered way out here in the middle of nowhere."

Jo, who owned Cup O' Jo's Café in the small town of Serendipity, Texas, sifted flour into a large bowl and then added baking soda and sugar. "Someone must think you're especially lovely, which, of course, you are."

"Eleven roses all together," Emily Richards replied as heat rose to her face. She pressed the fragrant bloom to her nose and inhaled the sweet fragrance. "I've received one every week since I came back from Ireland."

"Arriving by special courier, no less. I wonder how much it costs to get flowers transported to Serendipity?"

That was the least of Emily's questions. The single stems were delivered on the same day of each week to Cup O' Jo's, where she worked as a hostess. And each note was written in a hand she didn't recognize. She couldn't shake the feeling that the thoughtful gifts were tied somehow to her once-in-a-lifetime vacation to Ireland, but she couldn't imagine what the connection might be.

No one had ever sent her flowers before in all of her twenty-five years. No one.

"I honestly don't know," Em admitted, her voice soft and wistful. "I've never received flowers before, for obvious reasons."

Jo snorted. "Poppycock, girl. There's nothing less than perfect about you. Don't you go getting down on yourself. I won't hear of it."

Em smiled. It was impossible to stay melancholy around Jo.

"Now, let's figure out the mystery. I love a good puzzle. Weren't there any cards with the roses?"

"There were cards, but they weren't signed. I wish they were. That would make my life a great deal easier."

"Wouldn't it, though?" Jo pushed the large bowl of dry ingredients toward Emily. "Add the eggs and vegetable oil, if you please. So the cards were blank?"

"No, not blank. Cryptic." Em handed Jo the latest card, which included the words *the, road, back, fall*. "See? There are only a handful of words on each card, and they don't make any sense together. As far as I can tell, they have no relation to each other at all. I've tried rearranging the words and letters, but so far, I've got nothing. I have no idea what to make of it."

What, why, how – and most importantly, *who*.

"Roses have color meanings attached to them," Jo suggested, tapping her index finger against her chin. Emily passed the well-mixed batter back to Jo, and she folded in freshly sliced strawberries.

"I don't see how that could be. I've received roses in a number of colors. Yellow, pink, red and white."

"Friendship, admiration, love, new beginnings. If you ask me, that sounds like a message."

Emily blanched. She hadn't considered that the colors of the roses could convey special meaning, and the thought unsettled her. Was someone intentionally trying to jerk around with her emotions? As if her guard wasn't already as high as it could go. It wouldn't be the first time someone had played a mean-spirited trick on her.

But who? And why?

"These are Irish roses, my dear. It says so right on the back of the card. That can't be a coincidence. I do believe you made an admirer while you were on the Emerald Isle."

Emily gaped and shook her head. *Impossible.*

"You didn't connect with a young man while you were there?" Jo divided the dough between two loaf pans and placed them in the oven. "Be honest, now."

Heat that had nothing to do with the oven burned through Em, rising from the tips of her cowboy boots to her hairline. Her face flamed, and her cheeks had to be as red as fresh tomatoes.

Jo chuckled. "Oh . . . so there was somebody."

"No," Em said, but she'd hesitated a moment too long, and she knew from Jo's expression that she wasn't going to leave it be. She sighed. "Not like you mean, anyway."

Jo leaned her ample hip against the counter and reached for Em's hand. "You can tell me anything, you know."

Em nodded. She did know. Jo was one of the few people in her world who would really listen to her. Who would really care.

"Spill, girl. Who is he?"

"His name is Padraig O'Shea. I met him on the first day I was in Killarney. His parents own a plot of land that will someday be his. He's proud of his sheep farm and quite committed to working it. But most evenings he visits different pubs and taverns in the area to show off his skills as an Irish step dancer. The first time I saw him, I was mesmerized. It's breathtaking to watch two men dueling with each other through dance. He'd trodden his shoes so much he'd duct-taped them around the middle to keep them together."

"I've always thought those fellows were a strong and masculine bunch." Despite her advanced age, Jo giggled like a

219

schoolgirl. "Pounding out the rhythm in their hearts for all they're worth. What's not to like? So tell me all about Padraig. What did he look like? How did you meet him?"

"I was looking for a place to have dinner, and the pub next to my hotel, Fitzgerald's Tavern, came highly recommended for its fish and chips. That's also where I first tasted the strawberry soda bread similar to what we're making today."

"And you met Padraig."

"Not met, exactly. He was dancing in the after-dinner entertainment show. He's tall, with thick black hair and the biggest, kindest, brown eyes I've ever seen. When he looked at me, I melted right into them. And when he smiled . . ."

"You were a goner." Jo sighed dramatically and leaned her chin into her hand. "How romantic."

"I know it sounds crazy, but after the first time our eyes met, I felt like he was dancing just for me. Stupid, I know. But then he came off the stage and headed straight toward me. My breath hitched. I'm certain my heart stopped, only to start up again and beat overtime, when he asked me to come up on stage with him."

"You went on stage?" Jo sounded surprised, and Emily couldn't really blame her. It wasn't exactly feasible, even if that's exactly what had happened.

"I did. I couldn't believe it. I think I surprised myself most of all. He whirled me around until I was dizzy. Afterward, I waved to the audience, and everyone clapped for me. It was like a dream."

Jo pointed at the rose on the counter. "This dream apparently has some basis in reality. Did you see him again?"

"Every single night for the whole seven nights I was there," Em said with a laugh. "I'd sightsee in the daytime, but come evening, Fitgerald's lured me back in."

"I'm sure it was the superior fish and chips," Jo teased.

"Yes, I'm sure that was it."

"And this Padraig, he brought you back on stage?"

Em shook her head. "No. Just that one time. But every night after he'd finished dancing, he'd come sit with me. Most

220

nights we talked for hours. On the last evening of my trip he gave me a present, a framed print of an old Irish blessing. It's beautiful."

Her throat hitched. "I was sad to have to go."

"I'm sure you were. But can't you work something out? Surely with the Internet . . . And Ireland is only a plane ride away, albeit a long one."

"I know. And I hope to make it back someday. But my home is here, and he has his farm. Even if we wanted to pursue a relationship, it would be impossible."

"Nothing is impossible with God," Jo reminded her. "Life has a way of surprising you when you least expect it."

"You're talking about the roses."

"And the cards. You're sure you don't know what they mean?"

"No. I have no—" Her sentence dropped into silence as the realization hit her right between the eyes. The answer to her mystery was so obvious that she'd glossed right over it. She'd seen those words before.

Could it be? Were they from . . .?

"Jo, can you help me with something?"

Jo beamed at her. "Certainly, dear. What do you need?"

"Would you please reach my purse for me? It's over on the counter there. I've been carrying the rest of those cards around with me, hoping I could figure out what they meant. And now . . . well, after talking to you, I've realized I might know how to solve the puzzle."

Jo squealed with glee. "Oh, how delightful! I'm glad I can be a part of it."

Em wasn't even sure there was an *it*, not until she pieced the cards together.

"Do you have some scissors I could borrow?" she asked as Jo handed her the stack of cards. Her heart was beating a loud, erratic rhythm, her pulse roaring in her ears, as pure adrenaline took over.

With hasty, uneven clips, she cut the cards until each word was separated and then began reassembling them with shaky

221

hands.

Yes. There it was. The poem. The Irish Blessing Padraig had given to her.

May the road rise up to meet you,
May the wind be always at your back,
May the sun shine warm upon your face,
The rains fall soft upon your fields,
And until we meet again,
May God hold you in the palm of His hand.

It was there. All of it.

Everything except for the last two lines, which were noticeably absent. She figured they'd probably arrive with the next rose or two.

"I can't believe I didn't see this before," Em breathed in amazement. "Padraig has been sending me a message, and I didn't even know it." Her smile fading, she pressed her palm over her heart. "Well, not a message, exactly. More of a beautiful memory. I'll never forget that trip. I'll never forget *him.*"

"Don't you see, hon? He feels the same way about you."

Em was about to refute Jo's statement when the bell over the front door rang, indicating someone was entering the café.

"I thought you said you were closed for the day," Em said.

"I did," Jo said, her red eyebrows lifting. "It may be my nephew, Chance. Let me just take a peek around the corner real quick."

Jo bustled through the kitchen door, leaving Em temporarily alone. Her gaze returned to the words, now cut into pieces and rearranged in a way that made sense, and yet put together correctly, they formed the biggest mystery of all. Why was Padraig sending her flowers? What was with the cryptic messages?

"Uh, Em," Jo said when she reappeared, a gleeful light radiating from her eyes. "I think you're going to want to come and see this."

"This?"

Jo didn't elaborate, something that was very much — not Jo. The hairs on the back of Emily's neck prickled with apprehension. Jo was holding back, and she didn't know why.

"O . . . kay," she agreed hesitantly.

"Emily."

The rich, tenor voice came from behind her, over her left shoulder. The accent. The way only one person said her name.

Padraig?

Her heart seemed to stop beating, and she couldn't catch a breath. She couldn't move to save her life. She felt as frozen to the spot as an ice sculpture would be, and yet paradoxically, the warmth of Padraig's voice melted her bones and muscles into mush.

"Are you really here?" she asked without turning. She didn't want to look, afraid she was imagining his voice. His presence.

"I'm here." He chuckled. "Thanks in part to your friend, Jo. I couldn't have done it without her."

Jo was in on this? But how? Why?

"I couldn't stay away," Padraig explained, laying a gentle hand on her shoulder. "Jo helped me figure out a way to surprise you. Er . . . at least, I hope it's a surprise. I haven't been able to put aside our time together. You're all I can think about. I don't even know if you want me here, but I had to come, had to see if these feelings might be something we can build on."

Want him here? She'd never wanted anything more in her life. She placed her tiny hand over his large, roughened one, his touch reassuringly solid.

"I can't believe you're here," she said, her voice no more than a whisper.

"I figured it was my turn to cross the ocean." His voice lowered and gained a husky quality. "I felt I needed to deliver the rest of my message in person."

The rest of his message?

The poem.

Padraig reached for the arms of Emily's wheelchair and

turned her around to face him. The light in his eyes and the crease of his smile said more than words could, and he laughed as he spun her round and round. Then, his gaze turning serious, he crouched before her and took her hands in his, brushing light kisses over one palm and then the other.

"'And until we meet again, may God hold you in the palm of His hand.'"

A NOTE FROM DEB

This take on traditional Irish soda bread is delicious for breakfast or as a snack. My family has always been fond of banana and pumpkin breads. Strawberry soda bread is a wonderful addition to our collection of favorite recipes.

STRAWBERRY SODA BREAD

3 cups all-purpose flour
2 cups sugar
1 teaspoon baking soda
1 teaspoon salt
1 teaspoon ground cinnamon
1 ¾ cup vegetable oil
4 eggs
2 cups sliced strawberries

Preheat oven to 350 degrees. Grease and flour two 9x5x3 loaf pans. In large bowl, combine flour, sugar, baking soda, salt and cinnamon. Add eggs and oil. Mix well until batter is formed. Fold in strawberries. Divide batter between pans. Bake one hour. Cool in the pan for ten minutes. Turn bread out onto a wire rack. Let cool completely before slicing. For an extra treat, add 1 cup of chocolate chips or chopped nuts.

ABOUT DEB

Award-winning author **DEB KASTNER** writes Christian contemporary western romances. She lives on Colorado's beautiful Front Range with her husband and a pack of miscreant mutts. She has three grown daughters and two wonderful grandchildren. Spoiling the grandkids is her favorite hobby, but she also enjoys movies, music, reading and musical theater. Her latest Serendipity, Texas, novel is *Yuletide Baby*. Deb encourages her readers to "Love Courageously."

CHRISTMAS EVE GIFT

BY JOLENE NAVARRO

For all of her twenty-seven years, Ana Perez spent Christmas Eve on her Uncle Joe's ranch. Well, now it belonged to her cousins, but in her mind, it would always be Uncle Joe's. From where she stood at the kitchen sink, the huge window showcased the heart of the Texas Hill Country.

Maybe it was time to go somewhere different, see another part of the world. She loved Texas, but . . .

Large hands cupped her shoulders. Turning around, she found the warm blue eyes of her Uncle Norton staring down at her.

"Christmas Eve Gift!" He belted it as if calling to her from across the room. "Ha! I beat you this year."

"Christmas Eve Gift, Uncle Norton." She smiled and hugged him. Christmas Eve Gift was a silly game in her family with only rule. You had to be the first to say it. She wasn't sure were the tradition came from. It was one of those things you grew up thinking everyone did it, too.

"Here, let me take the bags." She looked inside. "Aunt

Peggy's pumpkin rolls. Christmas Eve has officially started."

Her uncle put his finger to his lips and pointed to the mudroom. Aunt Peggy was setting a pie on the counter.

At a volume that would make her Uncle Norton proud, Ana announced, "Christmas Eve Gift, Aunt Peggy!"

The petite redhead's hands jerked to her chest as she spun around, managing to set down the pie without dropping it. "Mercy me, girl. I thought everyone was in the living room or outside. Come here." The shorter woman wrapped Ana in a tight hug. "Christmas Eve Gift, dear." She looked at her bear of a husband. "Nortie, go get the gifts and the rest of the bags out of the Suburban."

"Yes, dear." He rolled his eyes, then kissed her on the forehead. "Like I don't know what my job is after thirty-two years of marriage."

Once her uncle left the room, her aunt turned on her, hands on hips and wearing a drill-sergeant stare. "Now what is that mopey face about?"

"I don't know what—"

"Don't pull that on me. This is your Aunt Peggy." She cupped Ana's face. "I know when something is bothering one of my chicks. Spill."

As much as Ana loved her family, sometimes they were just too much. Why did they feel as if they had the right to her every thought? "I guess I'm just missing Uncle Joe."

Her aunt went in for another hug and patted her back. "Oh, sweetheart, he made it very clear he wanted us to keep the tradition under his tree."

"I know. I just expect him to come down from the pump house or take the kids on a hike up the hill. It doesn't seem like he's been gone for almost a year."

Peggy nodded. "But there's more. What about you? We were so sure that Ethan would have a ring on your finger by now. He's not even here. Your mother's been very discreet about it, which is unlike her. So what's going on?"

Ana laughed. She tried to anyway. It sounded stiff even to her own ears. "I think she's in denial. Mom says we'll be back together as soon as I 'get over myself.'" She bit the inside of her cheek and shrugged, pretending it was not a big deal. She'd already spent too much time crying. "Aunt Peggy, he asked me to marry him, and I said no."

She gasped. "Ana Marie Perez, I . . . you really seemed to be perfect together. How could you tell that wonderful man no?"

"That's the problem. He's wonderful and perfect and . . ." She took in a deep breath and let it out in a heavy sigh. "Well, we know I'm not."

"Oh, sweetheart —"

"Christmas Eve Gift!" Isabelle stood in the doorway with hands high and her third-trimester belly protruding under a red Christmas sweater.

Hugs and greetings were exchanged. Ana rubbed her younger sister's belly. "You look like you're going to pop."

Laughing, Isabelle nodded. "I feel like I am, but the doctor says four more weeks. I can't wait to hold her in my arms."

Aunt Peggy kissed both sisters and went to supervise the placement of the gifts.

Isabelle leaned in close, reminding Ana of all the late nights and backseat secrets they'd shared over the years. "Ana, you should be warned. Mom has a surprise for you. I told her to talk to you, but you know how she loves dropping bombshells at unsuspecting victims."

Pressure pushed against Ana's eyes, the first signs of a monster headache. Please, not tonight. "I'm sure it can't be that bad."

"You just deserve a warning. Mom is determined to get you and Ethan back together."

"Oh, no. What has she done? She didn't buy us round-trip tickets to somewhere romantic, did she?"

"She might have, but it's worse than that. She—"

"Uncle Ethan!"

A chorus of all the children could be heard from the front door. Ethan's laughter blended with theirs. Ana's stomach turned over. No, her mother had *not* just brought him here. Not to their family Christmas Eve celebration.

She could sneak out the back door, get in her car and leave. Maybe head to the coast. She could go anywhere, anywhere other than the room where he was.

"Ana?"

His voice washed over her. He was at her back, but she could still see him. Tall, perfect lips, a crooked nose, a dimple that softened his hard jaw and hair that looked as if he'd just run his fingers through it. Dark hair that made his eyes look even greener. She would not turn around.

No more crying. She hated her mother's meddling. The back door was just a few feet away. It might be rude, but she could do this. It had broken her the first time she'd walked away from him. She wouldn't survive round two.

Isabelle caught her arm. "You can't just walk out."

"Yes, I can."

"Let her go, Belle. I thought your mother had told her."

How dare he be so nice and understanding? She clinched her fist and spun around. "I told you I didn't want to see you again. Did you think I lied?"

"Your mother said you didn't mean it and wanted to see me." He took a deep breath and shoved his hands in his pockets. "I missed you, but I'll leave if you want me to."

"No! Don't leave, Uncle Ethan." Cries came from the living room as the herd of kids rushed into the kitchen.

Piper, the smallest at five, grabbed Ethan's leg. "Aunt Ana, let him stay."

"Guys, it's okay," Ethan said. "Your gifts are already under the tree."

Katy, one of the teenage cousins, glared at Ana. "He shouldn't have to leave. Uncle Ethan is family. He said he'd take us up the hill."

Ana nodded. "They're right. You should stay. Everyone misses you. Christmas Eve Gift."

She had to get away from him and the way he looked at her, as if she was the only one who could fix his hurts. She couldn't be that person. Not any longer. He needed to move on and to find someone who could give him everything he deserved.

231

"Yay! Uncle Ethan, let's go." Tristan, at twelve, was the oldest boy.

Ethan gave Ana his "I'm-so-sad-and-adorable" smile. He eased closer, as if he was afraid she would bolt if he moved too fast.

"We need to talk."

"Have fun with my family. They love you. I said everything I'm going to say. I'm done."

"Fair enough. But I need *you* to hear a few things. I've had five weeks to think about everything you said. I might be slow, but I'm here now, and I need to say them."

"Uncle Ethan, we're waiting."

"We'll talk later." He went to kiss her on the ear like he used to whenever he left, but she pulled back. He didn't follow.

That was not disappointment in her gut. It wasn't.

Isabelle interlocked her arm with Ana's. "You still love him."

Her hushed whisper put to words Ana's deepest fear. She would never be over Ethan.

Two hours later, Ana was outside by the fire pit, her old, green, Army cot arranged so that the remaining orange coals could warm her feet. Her empty mug of hot chocolate rested on the ground next to her. On her back, she watched the sun get closer to the hills. The official watch would start soon. As a girl, she remembered begging Uncle Joe to proclaim the sun gone, the day over and the gifts to be opened.

She closed her eyes and listened to the sounds of the birds, deer snorting by the feeder and voices at the base of the hill. Ethan and the kids would be there soon, and all peace would be gone. She should have run when she'd had the chance. The voices faded again into silence, the only remaining sound from the occasional acorn hitting the metal roof. She was alone.

"Are you asleep on Christmas Eve?"

She startled at the sound of Ethan's voice. "You scared me."

"Guilty conscience?" He sat on the cot next to hers.

"How was the mountain?" She didn't want to think about her guilt.

"Missed you. Maybe next time you can go with us." He lay back with his hands behind his head, staring up at the same sky that she'd been watching. The sun shot the last rays of bold reds and yellows over the hills as the eastern sky pulled up a blanket of dark blue.

"Ethan, there won't be a next time."

"Five weeks ago I asked you to marry me."

"You seem to forget I said no."

"I remember. I'm just not buying your reasons. I know you love me."

She sighed loudly. "You know I can't give you a child."

"Yes, I know. But I won't let you decide *my* future out of fear. You know what I discovered this last month without you?"

Maybe if she ignored him, he would go away.

But he only continued. "I want you in my life. I want to hold your hand, kiss you, love you every day. Even at your worst, you're still the best thing I dreamed of having in my life."

"Ethan, you deserve to have a chance at being a father."

"Have you been in that house? We might never have our own child, but we'll never be childless. The world is full of people who have no biological children." He flipped over to his stomach and propped himself up on his elbows. "I want to hold you when you cry. I want to be the reason you laugh and smile." He reached across their cots and played with a strand of her hair. "Your smile is too beautiful to deny the world."

Ethan wanted to do this properly. Slipping off the cot, he lowered to one knee. "Ana, I can imagine a life without my own child. I can imagine us traveling the world, climbing the tallest peak and diving into the ocean. I can imagine all of that. What I can't imagine is a life without you. Please say you'll marry me. Watch the sun rise with me every morning. We'll gaze at the stars together every night. We'll dance together in the rain. Be my wife and let me be your man."

In the moonlight, he saw the moisture hovering on her lashes. When she shook her head slightly, his heart froze. What would he do if she said no again? He pressed his finger to her full lips. His mind searched madly for words that would keep her in his life, in his arms where she belonged. "Ana . . ."

Her eyes closing, she reached up to cover his hand with her own. He stopped breathing. His heart slammed inside his chest, begging her to accept him. She opened her eyes, and with a tentative smile, she nodded. Ethan blinked. She had *nodded.*

"I need to hear the words, Ana. Will you marry me?"

"Yes."

A roar came from deep in his gut. He threw his head back, wanting to beat his chest. All the worry and stress from the last month turned to absolute joy. The cot tilted as he pulled her close, wrapping his arms around her. The ground came up to meet them. He twisted so she wouldn't land on the rocks. They rolled a couple of times, laughing the whole time.

The back door opened, and the family rushed to them.

"She said yes!"

Ana wasn't sure which of the kids had said it, but they all jumped on top of them.

She laughed. "There goes our romantic moment."

Piper crawled over Ethan's shoulders. "Can we open the gifts now?"

Uncle Norton declared the day over, and everyone cheered. Just as fast as they had arrived, the family disappeared back into the house.

Ethan helped Ana off the ground and pulled her close. He pressed his cheek to hers. "We'll have a lifetime of romantic moments. Christmas Eve Gift."

A NOTE FROM JOLENE

With the birth of our first child, I started collecting Christmas Story picture books. On the first day of December each year, we would gather around the tree and read a couple of the books. Each night until Christmas Eve, the kids would pick different Christmas stories. This morphed into a family tradition that included hot chocolate and popcorn. This was a calm moment in the hustle of the holiday season. Grab a book, wrap up in fuzzy socks and comfy blankets and enjoy a mug of the best hot chocolate ever.

MEXICAN HOT CHOCOLATE

4 cups milk
1 cup water
¼ cup cornmeal *
1 to 2 cinnamon sticks
1/3 cup sugar
¾ teaspoon vanilla
4 to 6 pieces chocolate-baking bar (semi-sweet)

Combine milk, sugar, chocolate-baking bar and cinnamon sticks in pan over low heat until chocolate pieces melt completely. In a separate container, mix cornmeal and water. Dissolve any lumps. Add cornmeal mixture to milk. Stir or whisk over very low heat for 10 to 15 minutes. Milk will begin to thicken. Add pure vanilla extract after removing from heat. Whisk before serving to get a frothy topping.

* For a thicker drink, add more cornmeal.

ABOUT JOLENE

A seventh-generation Texan, **JOLENE NAVARRO** knows that though the world changes, people stay the same. Good and evil. Vow keepers and heartbreakers. Jolene married a vow keeper, who showed her that sweet kisses and dancing in the rain never get old. Her life, like her stories, is filled with faith, family and life's wonderful messiness. *Lone Star Holiday* and *Lone Star Hero* are currently available. Connect with Jolene at www.jolenenavarrowriter.com.

RECIPE INDEX

DESSERTS/TREATS

Made in the USA
Lexington, KY
27 September 2016